Gary McMillan

Tye Watkins in
SECOND
CHANCE
Book VII of the Tye Watkins Series

D1565629

Gary McMillan

1

Dedication

This book is dedicated to the memory of our son, Casey, who left us way too soon. We miss you very much.
Casey Jerrod McMillan

8/29/73-8/30/2010

Gary McMillan

Cover Concept & design by Michael McMillan

Copyright February 2011

ISBN Number 978-0-9844730-4-5

Published by Authors Discovery Cooperation, Inc.
4608 Clover Ave.
Odessa, Texas 79762

Printed in the United States of America

Second Chance

Tye Watkins is Chief of Scouts at Fort Clark, Texas. His father had been one of the original mountain men who had settled in Texas along the Border of Mexico after the beaver craze began to play out in the middle 1830's. He married and had a son named Tye in 1839. From the time Tye was old enough to walk, he had taught the boy to track, read sign, hunt, shoot, and every other skill a man would need to know to survive. When Tye was nineteen, his father was killed. Tye continued to hone the skills his father had taught him until he was considered one of the best scouts in the army. He was feared by the bandits, and because of his tracking and fighting skills, he was respected by the Apache as an equal which was unheard of for any white man.

Shakespeare McDovitt, nick-named Buff, was a seventy-one year old ex-mountain man. He was Tye's father's best friend when they trapped beaver together in the Rockies and the Yellowstone. He had come to Fort Clark to meet his old friend's son and had spent a great deal of time telling stories to Tye about his and Ben's time together in the mountains. He now lives on the fort with Tye and his wife, Rebecca.

Gary McMillan

Authors Note

Fort Clark was established in June of 1852 at Los Moras Springs by companies C and E of the First Infantry, under the command of Major Joseph H. LaMotte. The site was used for many years by the Apaches and was a stopping place for the Comanche on what was known as the great Comanche Trail going into Mexico. Fort Clark was located about thirty miles from the Rio Grande River, 32 miles east of present day Del Rio, Texas.

Due to its close proximity to the Mexican border, Fort Clark was the most active of all the border forts. During the Civil War all federal troops were pulled from the forts in Texas. With no troops to control them, bandits, Apaches, and the Comanches raised havoc along the border. After the war, troops once again came to Fort Clark in December of 1866 with orders to protect the military road to El Paso and to defend the settlers against Indian depredations, and the bandits that jumped back and forth across the Border.

The fort was officially closed in June of 1941 after almost 100 years of distinguished service. During its history, many famous military officers served there: Civil War heroes, Generals Sherman and Sheridan, Colonel Ranald S. Mackenzie during the Indian Wars, World War Two heroes, Generals Patton and Wainwright were all at Clark one time or another.

Many of the stone buildings built in the 1870's and 80's are still standing, in fact, many are being used. The two-story enlisted men quarters are now the fort's motel. The guard house is the museum. Officer's row is now two story homes to families on the fort and the commanding officers quarters is also home to a family. The wooden Palisades building, built in 1868, is still standing.

There is fishing, a golf course, hiking, biking, horse back riding, and a great museum of the history of this historic fort. Seven miles north is Alamo Village where more than a hundred western movies have been filmed, including John Wayne's, *The Alamo*.

Take the time to plan a trip and visit the historic old fort.

Books in the Tye Watkins Series

Border Trouble
The Crossing
Yancey
The Desperate Trail
Drums Along the Border
Back To the Rockies
Second Chance

Gary McMillan

Second Chance

Adam Carter was content being a cowboy, working cattle every day for the Rocking B Ranch. Over a period of time, he allowed 'so called friends' to convince him otherwise. Together, they robbed the owner of the ranch he worked for and in the process, killed the rancher's wife and son. Adam was on the run now with a new label…thief and murderer. He and his friends were headed for the safety of Mexico with the rancher on their trail intent on killing him.

Along the trail, the rancher crossed paths with Tye Watkins, Chief of Scouts from Fort Clark. After hearing the man's story, Tye joined the chase, hoping to intercept the outlaws before they crossed the Rio Grande and disappeared into Mexico.

Meanwhile, at Fort Clark, a young boy is almost beaten to death by a man just to steal the youngster's horse. The boy, fourteen year old Todd Jenkins, was Tye's nephew. Tye could be a man's best friend and would do anything to help that friend, but there was the other side of him-a dark side. When he lost his temper, neither his wife nor anyone else knew what he would do. They knew the scout could be as gentle and friendly as a lamb or he could become as mean as an Apache. One thing for sure, the man responsible for the beating was in trouble. The problem was, Todd was lying unconscious in the fort's hospital, and he was the only person who knew what happened.

While on the trail of the outlaws who killed the rancher's family and the man who beat his nephew, Tye encounters a large band of Comanche, an ambush by Mexican bandits, and an old enemy by the name of Horatio Alvarez also known as *The Ghost*, who is determined to kill the scout. The long and bloody trail finally ends with a strange twist, one Tye would never have expected.

Chapter One

Adam Carter squatted beside the small fire, his blanket pulled tight around his shoulders holding back the chill of a late fall night. He sat staring into the flickering flames, but not really seeing them. He was lost in his thoughts, trying to figure out how in the hell he had let his life come to this point. He had a lot going for him until four days ago. He was happy being cowboy, working on a ranch whose owner treated him as a friend, not an employee.

Adam was average in height, three inches short of six feet, and rather on the slender side. The ladies thought him to be handsome with his blonde hair and deep blue eyes. His parents were honest, hard working people and he was now a cowboy with the same work ethics. He had been riding horses since he was old enough to walk, and working cattle since he was fourteen. He was twenty-one years old, and already a top hand that could also do numbers and read writing well enough to get by. He was content being a cowboy for this sort of life was all he ever dreamed of. And now, that life was gone-he had another label, a thief and murderer.

He looked at the four men alongside him, all asleep in their bedrolls. It was common knowledge that his boss, like most ranchers, kept a good sum of cash in their home. These friends convinced him that he should rob his boss and they would help him. Bill Ross, owner of the Rocking B Ranch which was located a few miles southwest of San Antonio, employed him. Adam had worked there for over a year and was content, or so he thought; but one of his *"friends,"* Randy Neuman, had convinced him otherwise the last time Adam was in San Antonio on a Saturday after payday. He told Adam he was too smart to work for cowhand wages the rest of his life and be broke twenty-nine days of the month. *"Why I ever listened to those four I will never know,"* he thought to himself. *"If I was so smart, how in hell I let the likes of these four talk me into this mess is beyond me."*

Once a month like clock-work, Bill Ross would take two days and go to San Antonio for supplies. Adam, as did the other two hands on the ranch, knew the old man kept a large sum of cash in the house. Adam let himself be convinced by Randy and the other three, it would be so easy to take it while Ross was away and Mrs. Ross and their son were taking their daily morning ride. No one would get hurt.

The day Bill left for San Antonio; Adam's friends were a short distance away, watching the ranch. The two other hands worked north of the home two miles away. When the men saw Mrs. Ross and her son Jason leave, they rode into the yard where Adam was waiting. Adam, who was supposedly sick, did not go with the other hands. It only took a few minutes of ransacking the house to find the money.

The door opened unexpectedly and Jason and Betty Ross walked through the door. Jason, like most fifteen year old young men, carries a Colt on his hip. Seeing what was going on, the teenager reached for his gun. Randy was faster, and Jason was dead before he hit the floor. Betty screamed and reached for Jason's gun which had fallen from his hand to the floor, but she died with a hole in her forehead from Randy's pistol. Before leaving, the men removed several horses from the corral, and took the coffee, bacon, and biscuits that Mrs. Ross had made that morning.

Adam was in shock from the turn of events. The plan for a simple robbery had now become murder. Everyone would know he was involved, so he headed west, along with Randy and the others, toward Mexico and hopefully, safety. He knew Bill Ross would soon be on his trail. From what Ross's hands had told him, the old man was a hell of a tracker. Tracking Apache and bandits was what he had done when he was with the Rangers, and he was known for never quitting until the job was done. Adam figured with a simple robbery and not the killing, Ross might not have been so determined to leave his family for whatever time it took to track the thieves down. The killing of his wife and son would mean there would be no stopping him. He pulled the blanket tighter and stared at the fire. *"Damn you to hell Randy Neuman."*

~~

Bill Ross lay under his wool blanket shivering. He was fifty-five years old and the older he got the less tolerance his body had for cold weather. He wasn't a big man, standing five-six in his stocking feet, and weighing maybe one hundred and forty pounds. Years of riding in the wind and the Texas sun had his face and hands as dark and tough as the leather of his saddle. He was an honest man, and known to be a man of his word. A handshake was all any man needed from him. He looked folks straight in the eye and when he said he would do something; they knew he would do what it took to get it done. He was now camped here in the middle of nowhere, and miserable instead of comfortable in the warm bed at his ranch because he promised his wife on her grave that he would find the men responsible for their deaths.

The small fire had burned down to coals, but he lay there, not wanting to get out from under the blanket. A minute later he mumbled, "Ah hell," and rolled out of his bedroll. He added a couple of pieces of wood and in a few seconds, they burst into flames. He crawled back under the blanket and stared at the dark sky and let his mind wander back as to why he was here.

Three days ago, his world had been shattered when he had returned to his home from San Antonio. He owned a small spread about thirty miles southwest of town. The 'Rocking B' Ranch was small compared to some of the other spreads, but it was his and his wife's dream home. Her name was Betty Lou, and the ranch had been named after her.

When he returned, he was surprised to find his two hands in the yard, instead of working. Standing in the yard with his hands were three men he recognized, all being friends of his and fellow ranch owners. They all watched him as he rode into the yard and dismounted. He could tell by their expressions that something was wrong, and he immediately thought of his wife because she should have been out there also to meet him. As he walked up to the men he knew for sure something was wrong, they all were looking at the ground, not meeting his eyes.

He looked at Bill Gillespie who owned a ranch that bordered his on the east, and asked him what was going on. The rancher took off his hat, held it in front of him and told Ross what had happened.

Ross rushed into the house to find his wife and son lying side-by-side on the bed looking as if they were asleep. He had stood there like a statue, unable to move. The ranchers came into the bedroom, and each man saying something and patting him on the shoulder. Later, he could not recall what anyone said, because a million things were churning through his mind.

Finally, the two men who worked for him led him to a chair. One of the ranchers brought him a glass half full of whiskey. The burn of the whiskey brought him out of his dazed condition. Anger now began to replace the shock.

Bill, in his younger years, had ridden with the Rangers, or Texas Mounted Rifles as some called them. He had many a fight with Apache and outlaws and had developed a reputation as a man to ride the river with. He had fought and killed men, both red and white, but hate had never engulfed him. But now, he was feeling hate and seeking revenge. He trembled like he had a fever, and knew there was only one way to extinguish the fire was to track the bastards down that had done this terrible deed and shoot'um.

His good friend, Gillespie sat down alongside him and told him the house had been ransacked. His money box was gone and so were several horses from the corral. Furthermore, it looked as if his other employee, Adam Carter, was one of the men involved, if not the leader of the gang. Ross wasn't sure what he would do when he caught up with the gang other than kill Carter. He might get shot and die, but with his dying breath, he would kill that low-life sonofabitch. The man had not only killed his family, but had broken the code cowboys lived by, *riding for the brand*, which meant you were true to the rancher who paid your wages. Gillespie told him that the tracks indicated that five men were involved, counting Carter. Ross did not know who the others were, but it didn't matter. His other two hands, Wallace Anderson and Lester Hindman, both were old Ranger friends of his. He figured the three of them could handle ten of the likes of that bastard, Carter. As a Ranger, he always believed in quick justice and by God, it was damn sure going to be swift this time.

Gillespie and the others indicated that they would watch over the place while he was gone. They even offered to track the men, but Bill insisted he and his men could handle the killers. He thanked them for their kind offer. Gillespie and the others said the least they could do would be to keep an eye on the place while he was gone.

" *Maybe justice will come tomorrow,*" he thought as he drifted off to sleep.

~~

Tye was staring at the small fire in the distance. He knew what patrols were in the field, and none should be close to here. He suspected the fire was probably at least three or four miles away, but distances could be deceiving at night. He was curious as to who it could be. Apaches would not have a fire that visible, so it was either folks traveling looking to settle somewhere or it could be bandits crossing the Rio Grande from Mexico.

Todd Jenkins, Tye's nephew, and Dan August were camped with Tye on the side of a hill. Dan was the best of the scouts that worked for Tye as well as being a good friend. Todd was a fourteen year old young man that was Tye's mother's sister's son. His parents and sister had been murdered three months ago and Todd had been wounded. Tye tracked the killers down, who later had their necks stretched with a hangman's rope.

Tye had convinced Todd to stay at Fort Clark with Sergeant O'Malley and his wife until he decided what he wanted to do. He thought the young man should wait awhile and then return to his parents homestead and make a go of it. It was a nice spread and he told Todd he thought that is what his parents would have wanted. In the meantime, Tye had taken the young man under his arm, teaching him to track, hunt, read sign, shoot, and all the other things he would need to know to make it out here in this country. The land along the Border showed no mercy to man and could kill you as quick as an Apache arrow or a bandits bullet.

Dan looked at the flickering campfire in the distance. "Who do you think it could be?"

"It could be anybody but we both know it's not Apaches."

"How do you know," the always inquisitive Todd asked.

Dan answered. "Apaches know it is always better in this country for people not to know where you are. They would have a fire like ours, small and surrounded by rocks stacked to hide most of the flames. That's something you need to remember when you are on the trail in this country."

"We'll see if we can find out who it is in the morning," Tye said as he sat down on his bedroll next to the fire. Both, Dan and Todd sat down on theirs.

"Kinda chilly tonight isn't it? " Todd said holding his hands over the flames of the small fire.

"It's that time of the year," Tye said. "I remember about this time last year when I was chasing Yancey Cates up north of here. It was damn cold and a lot of snow."

"Did you catch him?" Todd asked.

Before Tye could answer, Dan said. "He caught the man and almost beat him to death before he brought him in."

"Why did you do that?"

Tye laughed and said, "The man wouldn't keep his foul mouth shut. He called me and the army just about every name in the book, and then he threatened to kill my wife. That was the wrong thing to do. I didn't kill him though, and he was hung shortly after I brought him in."

Tye stood up. "I'm going to check the horses." As soon as he walked away Todd asked Dan.

"Does everyone he goes after get killed or hung?"

Dan laughed and picked up a stick and stirred the fire. "That man is one in a million, Todd. There are a lot of good people moving out here, but there are also a lot of men just too lazy to work and want what those good people have worked for. There are men who are just evil, men who rob and kill people. It's this type of men Tye is sent after, just like the men who killed your parents and sister, and shot you. When Tye catches up with them, sometimes they are killed. I know Tye very well and have for a long time, and if he has one fault in his makeup, it's his fairness. He would never shoot a man from ambush. I don't like to do that either, but sometimes you have to protect yourself. I just hope that one fault doesn't get him killed one day. I'll tell you one thing Todd; you will never find a better man or friend than Tye."

Tye returned and sat down, looked at Todd and smiled. "Are you ready to continue your education in reading tracks?" Todd nodded and scooted closer to the scout.

Tye made a fist and using his knuckles, made some tracks on the ground. "What are these?"

Todd laughed. "Everyone knows a deer track."

Tye nodded. "That's true, but is it a buck or doe?"

Todd looked questionably at Tye, then at Dan. "How…how am I supposed to know that without seeing the deer?"

"That's part of reading sign, son." He picked up a stick and pointed at the two tracks on the left, one in front and one behind. "See how the rear track is inside of the front one?" Todd nodded.

"That's a buck. He pointed to the other set. "See where the rear track is outside the front track?"

"Yes sir."

"That's a doe."

"Oh," Todd said, nodding his head. "I'll remember that."

"What is the first thing you look at when reading animal tracks," Dan asked?

"The shape and whether it has claws or not," Todd answered. Then he added, "If it doesn't have claws, then how many toes does it have. A deer, buffalo, and wild hogs have two. A dog, coyote, wolf, and fox have four but will usually leave claw marks. A panther or bobcat will have four toes, but most of the time the claws or retracted and don't leave a mark. Animals like skunks, badgers, weasel, and bears have five toes with claw marks showing."

"Damn, Tye." Dan said laughing. "You're teaching this youngster well."

Tye nodded. "He's a quick learner. I've been waiting a long time to teach someone like him the things my pa taught me. I intend to do it with my son when he is old enough, that is if it is a boy."

"What if it's a girl," Todd asked?

"She'll grow up to be a lady like her mother." Then he laughed and added, "But then again, I may teach her how to use her fist so she might just be able to whip any man around." He lay down on his bedroll and pulled the wool blanket up to his chin. "Let's get some sleep."

Chapter Two

The morning dawned clear and cold, so the outlaws lay huddled in their bedrolls. Finally, realizing they were making a mistake by not already being on the trail, they pulled their boots on and saddled their horses. Adam had told them about his boss's being an old Ranger and each figured that by now, he was on the trail. He would probably have the other two men who worked for him with him.

Mounting their horses, they rode west with the stolen horses. Adam figured they were still two days from the border, two days of looking over his shoulder and wondering if he was in the old man's rifle sights. Adam was twenty-one and had never been on the run before. Hell, as far as he knew he had never broken any law. Now, he was wanted for robbery and murder. He reached up and touched his throat, pondering what a rope would feel like. He had heard all kinds of horror stories from men who had witnessed a hanging. Sometimes, it was quick. Other times, if the hangman didn't figure things just right and it didn't break the man's neck, the man choked to death. There were even stories of a man's head being torn from his body. He looked at the horses they had taken and shook his head. You could also add horse stealing to the list.

The morning air was still cold, but Adam found himself beginning to sweat.

~~

   Tye, Dan, and Todd broke camp just as the eastern sky was turning gray. They had ridden to within a half mile of the fire they seen last night, and saw men leaving the camp. Tye, looking at the men with binoculars, said they looked like cowboys driving some horses. The fort had no reported horses stolen, so he let it go without another thought. They swung left intending to go by Tye's old homestead. He would do some repairs on the house and spend some private time at his parent's graves. Every time he was in this part of the country he stopped. If a person didn't know, he would think someone still lived there because of the upkeep Tye did.
   They stopped about noon in the shade of a cliff where a small patch of grama grass grew. After loosening the girths on the saddles, they let the horses graze while the men chewed jerky.
   "We've got company, Tye," Dan said nodding toward the east. Tye looked and saw three riders about a quarter mile away. One never knew what to expect in this country, but a wise man always expected the worse. They tightened their girths on the saddles, mounted, turned and faced the riders. Tye and Dan both had Henry repeaters lying across the saddle in from of them,

fingers on the triggers. Todd was told to stay behind them. The approaching men pulled up about fifty yards out and sat looking at them.

A long moment of silence passed before one the men came forward, hands away from the gun holstered on his hip. The man's rifle was in the saddle scabbard, so Tye relaxed a little, but still kept his finger close to the trigger and the barrel pointed in the general direction of the man.

"Bill Ross of the Rocking B spread southwest of San Antonio," the man yelled. "Who am I speaking with?"

Tye kicked Sandy and moved a few steps closer, finger still on the trigger and one eye on the men behind the lone rider in front. "Tye Watkins," he said.

The man straightened up. "The scout at Fort Clark?"

Tye nodded and the man twisted in the saddle. "Its okay, come on up," he said to the others. Ross stepped from the saddle, dropped his reins and walked toward Tye, Dan, and Todd. Tye dismounted, the Henry still in his left hand.

The rancher spoke to the two riders when they arrived. "This here is Tye Watkins, the scout at Fort Clark." Both men recognizing the name, looked at Tye, and nodded.

Ross said, "This here is Wallace Anderson and Lester Hindman. They work for me." Tye looked at the men, especially Anderson. The man looked about the same age as Ross. Both of the men with Ross had the look of individuals who had seen trouble before and handled it. Tye was good at sizing folks up and he knew both of these men had been "up the river and around the bend" before. .

Tye looked again at Anderson. "Do I know you?"

Anderson dismounted and walked over to Tye sticking out his hand. "I rode with you and your pa for a short time with the Rangers but that was a long time ago. It's good to see you again, Tye." Tye shook his hand.

"Good to see you again too." Tye turned to the older man. "You're a long ways from your ranch Mr. Ross. What brings you out here?"

"Chasing some men, Tye-men that murdered my wife and son four days ago. They took all my money I had in my home plus several horses."

"Were there five men?"

Ross's head snapped around. "How did you know that?"

"Last night we saw a campfire some ways off. We knew it wasn't Apaches. We came on their camp this morning as they were riding away west, toward Mexico. I watched through my binoculars and saw there were five of them plus eight or ten horses. We have had no report of any trouble so I didn't think much about it."

"How far behind are we?" the man named Hindman asked.

"From where we are, maybe five or six hours."

The three men mounted their horses. "Let's ride," Ross said.

Tye grabbed the man's reins. "Hold on just a second." He turned to Dan. "Take Todd back to the fort. Tell Major Thurston what happened, and ask him to get a patrol in the field. Bring them here and pick up our trail." He turned to the three men. "If it's okay with you, I would like to trail along and see if we can catch them before they get across the Rio Grande into Mexico."

"Get mounted, Tye. You're more than welcome." Ross reached down and shook Tye's hand. For the first time, the rancher felt like they might have a chance to catch the men before they crossed the Rio Grande into Mexico.

Tye mounted Sandy, and then shook Dan's and Todd's hands. "Todd, you tell Rebecca where I went."

"She gonna be mad?"

"No Todd," Tye said laughing. "She knows me and knows how I am. I'll see you in a few days." Tye turned and with the others, rode west.

Todd watched them leave. "What did he mean by 'Rebecca knows me and how I am'?"

Dan hesitated, getting his thoughts straight before answering. "She knows Tye will not stand for men robbing or killing people. Everyone knows he will do all he can, even risking his own life, to protect them. Like I told you before, Todd, he's one in a million. I've been here all my life, chased robbers and murderers, fought Apaches, and thought I knew it all, till I met Tye. He's taught me more in two years than I had learned in my whole life, and not just about scouting. He's taught me how to be a man, and what life is about. You may not know this but he is a deeply religious man. He's the best scout in the army. He can kill a man a hundred different ways. He will risk his life for a friend. He is a wonderful, loyal husband and when the baby is born he will be a great father. You won't meet another like him in your lifetime, so enjoy him, learn from him, and one day you can tell your children that you knew him." Both nudged their horses into a gallop.

~~

Ross and his men were running their horses too hard and Tye had to make them slow their mounts to a trot.

"We ain't gonna catch them bastards at this pace," Hindman said.

"You'll play hell catching them on foot Lester," Tye said. "If you keep running these horses like you were that's exactly where you will be. Trust me. I know this land and I know where they are headed. We can take a short cut and maybe make up three hours on them."

"Tye's right, men." Ross said. "We go off half cocked and we'll lose them for sure." He looked at Tye. "We're with you Tye. Just lead the way."

Tye nodded. "Let's go then."

~

Adam and the others paused at mid afternoon to rest the horses, grab a quick bite of jerky and determine how far they were from Mexico. The only one who had been here before was a man named Matt. He thought they were a day, maybe a day and a half from the border. He also told him there was only one place to cross for several miles. Matt then went on to talk about the senoritas in the cantinas.

Adam stood up. "That all sounds good, Matt, but we have to get there first. I can promise you old man Ross is back there, and he's coming hard. We need to move and keep our eyes open."

"It's been four days, Adam. Don't you think he would have caught up by now if he was coming? It's not like we have been setting a fast pace. I think you over estimated that old man."

"Maybe, but I don't think so. I was around him just about every day for a year or so. I think I know him. Hell man, we killed his wife and son. Would you quit if you were in his place? Besides, he was not due back till the next day after we left. He would also have to bury them before he left so I figure it was a day and a half or maybe two days before he started after us. I figure he's a day or less behind us."

Neuman stood up. "Maybe you are right, maybe you are wrong. I don't know, but I am going to play it safe and move." He stepped into the saddle. "Ya'll coming or staying?" The others mounted their horses and continued toward Mexico, Matt leading the way.

~~

Back at Fort Clark, Rebecca had just left the fort's hospital. Everything was fine, and she should expect the baby in two or three weeks. Mrs. O'Malley had gone with her. She watched over Rebecca like a mother hen, spending hours telling her what to expect during childbirth.

"Everything okay, Rebecca," Buff asked when she came through the door?

"Doc said everything is as it should be, Buff. It should be a couple weeks." She walked around the table and sat down next to the tough old mountain man. "You're going to make a great grandpa, Buff."

"Well, I don't know about that, but this old codger is sure going to give it a good try. I have never held a baby you know. Don't know if I can or not. Be scared to death I might drop it."

Rebecca laughed. "You won't drop the baby, Buff. Nature will take over and you will do fine."

"I hope so. But I get all knotted up in my gut when I think about being a grandpa and holding that tiny thing. I may be more nervous than Tye when the time comes."

Rebecca stood up and kissed Buff on the top of the head. "You will be great Buff. Quit worrying about it." She patted him on the shoulder. "I think I'll lie down for awhile before fixing dinner. Wake me in a couple of hours."

"Shore enough, Rebecca." Buff walked outside and sat down on the porch. *"This getting to be grandpa is going to take some getting use to,"* he thought. *"I figure my old trapping buddy Jim Bridger would get a laugh if he knew about it. I was happy back in those mountains trapping beaver even though it was tough. That is what I wanted to do and I thought I was as happy as a man could get- but I ain't so sure now. The last few months living here and seeing how happy Tye and Rebecca are with her being pregnant, living in a nice home and around people I like is making me think I missed out on a lot of what life is all about. I had forgotten how it felt to live in a home, be around people you cared for, and them caring for you. It's a good feeling. Yep, I'm going to be the best damn grandpa that ever lived and I'm going to spoil that kid something fierce."*

He laughed out loud at that thought. He stood up and stretched, *"yes sir,"* he thought, *"things are going to be alright."* He walked toward Los Moras Creek and his favorite tree and sitting down, leaned back and closed his eyes.

Chapter Three

Tye held the horses to an easy gallop for about three miles, slowed to a trot, and then walked the horses for thirty minutes before galloping again. He knew Sandy could do this all day. He looked at the other men's horses and was pleased at what he saw. *"One thing you could count on was a rancher having good stock,"* he thought to himself.

"How are we doing?" Bill asked.

Tye gave the tough old coot a smile. "I think we'll catch up with them at first light if you three are willing to push it for a while after dark." He looked back at the other two men.

"Let's get this thing over with," Lester said. "We'll stay with you, Tye."

Bill Ross smiled. He had known these two for a long time, and knew they could be counted on in a pinch. They worked for him, but they were also his friends and he knew a man didn't have many of them. A man would have many friends during his lifetime, but how many could he count on when push came to shove-not many, maybe two or three if he was lucky-he felt he was lucky.

"Tye, I haven't seen any tracks lately," Wallace said.

"We left the trail awhile back," Tye said. "Right now, we're on the shortcut I told you about. We should come out about a mile above the crossing, and hopefully we can be in position there before they arrive." Tye settled his butt firmly in the saddle. "Let's go." They had been walking their mounts, and now he led them away at a canter that the horses could hold for miles. He knew though, that the terrain would change from the rolling hills they were in now as they got closer to the border. The horses would be walking then because of rocks, ravines, cliffs, and thick stands of sage and mesquite.

~~

Adam had made up his mind he was going to leave this crazy bunch of men the first chance he got. It was apparent they were following Neuman and would listen to no one else. He also figured they were going to do some crazy things in Mexico, and then they would have the damn Federales on their tails. He would break away as soon as they crossed the border and head north, holding close to the Rio Grande before crossing back into Texas. The only thing he worried about was reaching the damn river alive, so he could carry out his plan.

Second Chance

It was getting late and they were seeking a place to camp. Earlier, Neuman had sent the man named Garrett back to see if he could spot anyone following them. The terrain had changed the last two miles. They were now in steep hills and rocky ground with sparse patches of grass.

"About a mile ahead," Matt said, "There is a small cave close to a spring that usually has water. We should get there just before dark. If I recall correctly, there will be enough grass for the horses."

"Can Garrett find us after dark?" Adam asked.

Matt nodded. "He can follow tracks better than most. He'll find us."

Nothing else was said for a few minutes until Matt exclaimed, "There's the cave," as he turned toward the base of a cliff. They found the spring Matt had mentioned and there was sufficient grass to hold the horses. With water and grass here, the men were not worried about them wandering off. They had thrown their bedrolls in the cave and had a small fire going when they heard the clicking of horse's hooves. They had pulled their guns when a voice rang out.

"Its Garrett-don't shoot!"

"Come on in," Neuman said.

Garrett came into the light of the fire and dismounted. "Nothing back there I could see."

Neuman looked at Adam. "Looks like you were scared for nothing," a touch of sarcasm in his voice. The other men looked at Adam.

"Never said I was scared, Neuman," he said. "There's a difference between being scared and being careful. I said I figured he would be back there dogging us. Maybe I was wrong-maybe I wasn't."

"What do you mean by that?"

"Ross and the two men that worked for him were all Rangers like I said before. They've been all over this country and they may know a short cut to the crossing. Matt said there was only one place to cross. Is that right, Matt?" Matt nodded his head. Adam added, "I just don't think we should relax yet. That's all I've got to say." He sat down on his bedroll with his legs crossed, Indian style. No one said anything for a few seconds.

Finally Nate, who rarely said anything, spoke up. "Maybe Adam is right and maybe he is not, but if he is right, we might just walk into a trap. I say let's go on the basis he is and just be damn careful." Matt and Garret nodded their agreement and Neuman, seeing this spoke up.

"I personally think he is full of horse shit, but we will play it his way. One of us will be on sentry duty tonight, and we will be careful when we approach the crossing. Let's get something to eat, and get some sleep."

Second Chance

~~

Tye was true to his word about night riding. The sun had dropped behind the hills an hour earlier, but he kept the horses moving. Tye kept Sandy in the direction he wanted to go, but let the horse pick his way. Horses could see a lot better at night than a man.

"How much longer we going to ride, Tye?" Ross asked.

"We should be where I want to be in about two hours, maybe less. I'm pretty sure what crossing they are headed for. If I'm right, we'll be a little closer than they are. So far, they seem to be in no hurry, so if we get an early start, we'll get ahead of them and maybe surprise them."

They continued riding in silence for a few minutes before Bill spoke. "Just wanted you to know how much I appreciate you taking the time to help us out, Tye. It's not your fight or your problem."

"My pa frequently told me that it was a man's responsibility to help his neighbor. It's also my responsibility as Chief of Scouts at Clark to keep the people that live out here as safe as possible." Tye laughed and added. "That's a lot of words to just say... you're welcome". Bill laughed and looked back at Wallace and Lester. Both men had grins as wide as Texas. "I'll tell

34

you something you already know, Bill. You're fortunate to have men like Lester and Wallace riding for you. They will stand by you when things get tough. I have soldiers that are like that and believe me, when thing get crazy, it's a good feeling to have men you can trust to be there." Wallace and Lester looked at each other, grinned, and sat a little straighter in the saddle.

An hour later, Tye called a halt. He had found the spring. Lester and Wallace looked at each other, both wondering how in hell he found it in the dark.

"There should be some good grass here," Tye said. He looked around and added, "We'll need to keep a man on watch tonight. Apaches don't usually wander around in cold weather, but you're never sure what they are going to do. They know where this spring is. I've stayed alive out here by taking nothing for granted and always expecting the worst." He stepped from the saddle and smiled as he watched the three men stretch and walk around after their long hours in the saddle. "Let's water the horses, picket them and make some coffee and heat some biscuits.

"I'll take care of Sandy for you," Wallace said, taking Sandy's reins from Tye's hand.

"Thanks, Wallace," Tye said, and immediately begin piling some rocks in a circle to build a fire inside them. Bill brought some wood and Lester had a coffee pot filled with water. Tye took his knife and cut the wood into smaller pieces that would fit inside the ring of rocks. They quickly had a fire going, and in a few more minutes they poured the coffee grains into the boiling water. That wonderful aroma of fresh coffee immediately filled the air. Whether it was cowboys, soldiers, or outlaws, the aroma of fresh coffee pleased everyone. Bacon was put in a skillet and placed over the fire. When the bacon was ready, biscuits were dipped in hot grease; a feast for a king-if you haven't eaten all day, and hungry enough to eat the leather soles of your boots.

Lying in their bedrolls, the small talk commenced.

"How old are you, Tye?" Bill asked.

"Thirty," Tye answered. He chuckled and added, "A hard thirty."

The men all laughed and when it quieted down Wallace spoke. "I hated hearing about your pa getting killed, Tye. He was a good man and all the men in the Rangers respected him."

"I appreciate that, Wallace."

"Another thing," Wallace added. "I hear you took his place and did a great job."

Tye shrugged. "No one man could take pa's place and I didn't want to. I just took the things he taught me and did the best I could."

"From what I hear, that's an understatement," Lester said. Never one to like talking about himself, Tye could see where the conversation was headed so he quieted down.

"Let's get some sleep," Tye said. "Who has the first watch?"

"I do," Bill grunted. "Lester has the second and Wallace the third."

Tye turned to Wallace. "Wake me and I'll stand the last watch."

"One more question, Tye. How old were you when you killed your first Apache."

"Fourteen," Tye said as he turned on his side, his back to the men and mumbled, "Let's get some sleep."

The three men looked at each other shaking their heads all thinking the same thing. This man fought the Apache almost daily for sixteen years, and he is still alive. Silence fell on the camp as Bill took the first watch. The thought of Tye killing a man, an Apache, at fourteen years old had Bill thinking about what he was doing at that age.

"I was in love with a girl who lived a couple miles from our farm. Mary Ann Williams was her name. She was a cute little filly and we had a good time. I remember she liked to fish as much as I did, and we spent a lot of time on the creek banks with those sticks we used as poles. We never caught much but had a good time. I wonder where she is now. I guess I was like most boys that age, playing and chasing girls when I wasn't helping pa on the farm. I sure never thought about killing anyone and no one was

trying to kill me. That man lying over there never had a childhood. He probably never had a store bought toy in his life. Being the only child, he was never around kids much either. Fourteen and fighting Apaches while I was pulling on girls ponytails."

Bill glanced again over at Tye. *"Damn,"* he thought, *"fourteen and already fighting to survive."* He pulled the blanket a little tighter around his shoulders, leaned back against a boulder and stared off into the darkness. He thought of his wife and son and how life would be without them. A place like the Rocking B had been their dream for years. It would be an empty dream now. His emotions had run their course, and the tears had dried up. They had been replaced by hate, and a need for revenge. He wanted to kill a man, and the thought of his hands around the man's neck, squeezing the life out of him was overwhelming. In fact, he was afraid that the burning desire to kill a man would condemn him to hell. But he remembered somewhere in the Good Book something about *"an eye for an eye."* He stopped thinking and listened. "I'd better concentrate on the job at hand," he mumbled to himself.

He again pulled the blanket a little tighter and listened to the night sounds. He learned a long time ago to do that. Once your senses became accustomed to the normal sounds, a different sound would immediately get your attention. Doing this had saved his hide a couple times when he was a Ranger. Right now though, there were no sounds but the horses munching the short grass.

~~

Things were not so quiet back at Fort Clark. Dan and Todd had arrived and reported to the Post Commander, Major Thurston, about what Tye was doing. Thurston listened to the report, but knew there was nothing he could do to help Tye. Another problem had come up just before Dan came into his office; a report of a band of twenty or so Apaches had hit two homesteads near the junction of the Pecos River and the Rio Grande. Thurston was in the process of placing a large patrol in the field led by Captain McClellan to verify the report and if true, track the Apaches down and put an end to the problem before it got worse. He wanted his best scout leading the patrol, but with Tye gone, it was Dan.

"I have two patrols out already, Dan," Thurston said. "With the patrol that I am putting in the field at first light, I'm going to be short of men. I hate to say this, but Tye will have to make do on his own this time. Since you are Tye's best scout, I want you scouting for Captain McClellan." Dan knew the major well enough that it would do no good to argue.

"I'll be ready in the morning, Sir." He and Todd left headquarters. Dan headed toward his home and Todd towards Tye's.

Todd visited Rebecca and Buff before going to the O'Malley's place. He told her what had happened and that Tye and the rancher were chasing the killers. Todd then excused himself and left for the O'Malley's.

Rebecca sat down in a chair, her face in the palms of her hands and sobbed. Buff came over and put his hand on her shoulder.

"It will be okay Rebecca. You and I both know he had no choice. Tye has several hundred square miles to cover, a great number of homesteaders, and two hundred troops he is responsible for. When something happens like it just did to that rancher, Tye wants to catch the men who did it before they rob and kill someone else. Tye could be known as The Guardian of the Border."

Rebecca looked up and forced a smile. "How is it you never married? Ever since you have been here, every time I get down in the dumps, you have the words to pick me up. You could charm any girl you met."

Buff scratched the back of his neck and sat down in the chair next to Rebecca. "Never figured myself as a ladies man. Wasn't many ladies in those mountains you know," he chuckled.

"There were some Indian ladies weren't there?"

"Never was interested in marrying one."

"Did you ever…," she stopped. "I need to get us something to eat." She went to the stove. Buff was glad that conversation was over with because he knew what she was going to ask. He walked outside and sat down on the porch just as Senior Master Sergeant O'Malley arrived.

"What brings you over here, Sergeant O'Malley?"

"How's Rebecca? I haven't seen her lately."

"She's fine, Sergeant. Fine as a lady can be that's as far along as she is."

"Good. Tell her I said to come by the house. That woman of mine feels she needs to see her every minute of the day." He stood up. "Gotta run, Buff." He turned to leave, and then looked back. "I almost forgot. The missus wants you and Rebecca over tomorrow about six for supper if it's okay."

Buff nodded. "I'll tell Rebecca."

~~.

Tye had Ross and the men up an hour before first light. He told the men to keep the talk to a minimum and speak low if they needed to say anything. The ground was rocky and the horses made enough noise as it was. Tye figured they would reach the crossing about an hour after the sun was up and hoped he had guessed right about where the outlaws were headed.

"I hope they stopped to camp for the night," he thought. *"I would not have if I was in their place but these men, for some reason, have not seemed to be in a hurry. I guess they think no one*

41

is after them or they are just stupid. I think maybe it's stupid because how can any sane man think that a man who you just murdered his wife and son would not come after you. If I was them, I would have been in a mad rush and would have been in Mexico yesterday or before. Their taking their time like they have been is just stupid, or maybe arrogant."

The sun was breaking over the hills when Tye saw a cliff about two miles in front of them with a white streak running down its face resembling like a lightning bolt.

He turned to Bill. "The crossing is just to the left and a mile past that cliff yonder with the white streak on it."

"I see it."

"When we get there, you and your men stay out of sight while I mosey down see if anyone has crossed in the last few hours. If the men we are after happen to arrive while I'm down there, I could be just another cowboy on the trail like they are, and they shouldn't think much about it."

Bill nodded and asked. "What's the plan if they do arrive while you are down there? Are we going to let them pass on by or what?"

Tye thought for a moment. He turned in the saddle so the other two could hear him. "If they do come while I'm down there, I will keep some distance between myself and them. You have your rifles on them while I am talking. If I can convince them they are surrounded maybe we can end this thing with no one getting killed. If I scratch the back of my neck, the three you fire a shot in the dirt just in front of their horses. You will be spread out some so maybe shots coming from different directions will convince them they are surrounded. If it doesn't, and you see me leaving the saddle in a hurry, shoot to kill. We can hope they won't show up while I'm down there."

~~

The outlaws were awakened by Neuman before daylight. Neuman had been mulling the things Adam had said over in his mind and something told him that the kid might be right.

" *That old geezer just might be coming and hadn't showed up because of the late start like Adam said. The other thing about a shortcut could be true also.*" He had heard stories about the Rangers and knew they were smart and tough when they were on a trail.

They saddled their horses in the dark and rode out, hoping to be at the crossing in a couple of hours. Matt was leading the way. An hour and a half later they topped a hill over looking the crossing.

"There it is," he said, pointing.

Smiles crossed all the men's faces as the worry of being caught before they got here disappeared. They rode up beside Matt and looked at the crossing in the distance as the stolen horses began walking down the hill to the river.

When they hit the bottom of the hill a rider suddenly appeared. "Who the hell is that? Adam, is that one of the hands?" Neuman asked.

"No. I never saw him before."

"May be just some dumb cowboy headed to see the senoritas in Mexico," Matt commented.

"Maybe," Neuman said. "Let's go, but keep your hands close to your guns."

Tye saw the riders at the same time they saw him. "Damn the luck," he mumbled. Only thing to do was to play out the hand and see what happens. He kicked his moccasin boots out of the stirrups in case he had to leave Sandy's back in a hurry. He turned Sandy to face the men with a smile on his face.

"Who are you?" the man in front asked, being about thirty feet distant.

"Just a cowboy minding his own business like you should be doing."

"You talk pretty tough for a hombre that's outgunned five to one," the man answered.

"What makes you think I'm alone?"

Neuman and the others glanced around. "Looks to me like you are, and now… you are in a hell of lot of trouble." He leaned forward in the saddle and spoke again. "Now, one more time, what is your name?"

Tye slowly moved his hand from the saddle horn closer to his pistol. "My name is Watkins…Tye Watkins."

The name didn't register with Neuman, but it did with Adam and Matt. Matt asked. "You the Watkins from Fort Clark…the scout?"

"The same," Tye answered. The four of the men spoke among themselves, Tye being unable to make out what they were saying. The fifth man, for some reason, hung back, away from the others.

Finally, the man who had been doing most of the talking muttered. "So you are the famous scout who has the whole damn country wondering you're something not of flesh and blood." He leaned to his right and spat saying, "Well you have bit off more than you can handle this time, Mr. Famous Scout!"

"Before you do something foolish, I told you I was not alone." Tye scratched the back his neck with his left hand and three rifle shots kicked up dirt and rocks in front of the men. Their horses, startled at the shots, pranced back and forth, one bucking.

"It seems to me that you are the fellows who robbed a ranch southwest of San Antonio, killing a lady and her son, and then stealing some horses with the 'Rocking B' brand on them. And unless I'm blind, those horses over there appear to have the 'Rocking B' brand on them. Do you have a bill of sale?" He waited for a couple of seconds. "One of those men in the brush is the owner of that ranch as well as the husband and father of the two people you killed. Right now, you and two of the others are in their sights, and not many men are going to miss with a Henry rifle at forty or so yards." Tye could see the look on the man's face, a look of a desperate man. He had seen it before. He looked into the man's eyes and knew the outlaw was going to draw his gun, and men were going to die.

Chapter Four

Neuman, just as Tye figured, reached for his gun. Tye pulled his own weapon as he leapt from the saddle. Neuman was quick, and as Tye left the saddle, a bullet cut the air where he was an instant before. Tye hit the rocky ground hard and rolling, came up firing his pistol at Neuman. His bullet hit the man in the chest. An instant later, another bullet, one from the rocks, knocked him out of the saddle.

Complete mayhem started after the first shot. Tye kept moving sideways, firing at another outlaw but missing. His next bullet hit the man in the left shoulder. The man grabbed his shoulder, laid low in the saddle and kicked his horse, heading it toward the river. Tye dived to his left to keep from being run over, hitting hit the rocky ground hard. Shots were still being fired as he lay there. The man he had shot in the shoulder was on his horse forty yards away in the middle of the river. Tye raised himself on one knee, leveled his pistol, aiming just above the man's head, squeezed the trigger. An instant later, the man threw his hands into the air and tumbled backwards off his horse, into the river.

Tye moved sideways to face the other men. There was no one in the saddle to shoot. One was slumped over his saddle and another was lying on his back, his foot hung up in a stirrup being dragged slowly by his horse. Another man sprawled face down in the dirt. A fifth man was a quarter mile away riding like the devil. Tye turned and waded into the river to get the man he had shot. After reaching the man, he grabbed hold of the dead man's collar, and headed toward the bank.

Upon reaching the bank, Bill and the other two were nowhere to be seen. Fearing the worse, he left the dead man on the bank and entered the brush where Ross and the others were. Reaching the spot, he stopped. Wallace was sitting on the ground with Bill's head in his lap. Lester was standing beside Wallace, holding his shoulder, blood running through his fingers. Tye kneeled down and looked at Bill's wound. At first, he though it was bad. He was hit high in the right side of his chest. Tye noticed there was no blood bubbling from his lips indicating the bullet probably missed his lungs. That was a good sign. He rolled the old man on his side and saw the exit hole which was good, because he would not have to suffer Tye digging the lead out.

"He going to be okay, Tye?" Wallace asked.

"I think so. There is no bloody froth coming from his lips so the bullet apparently missed his lungs, which is good. We need to get him to the old sawbones at Fort Clark. He'll never make it if you try to take him anywhere else because of the distance. The fort is less than a day's ride and the surgeon there will fix him up. He then looked at Lester's shoulder. The bullet had just creased him, leaving a gash across his shoulder. It was bloody and would be sore, but it was not serious.

Tye looked at Wallace. "Why don't you take a look at the dead men and see if your co-worker is among them. I'll doctor Lester and Bill the best I can and then you can get them to the fort. I'll go after the other man when you are headed back.

Minutes later, Wallace returned mad as hell. "That damn Adam was not one of them. He was the one that ran away…running like the coward he is."

Tye walked over to the dead men's horses and rummaged through the saddle bags. He found a bag with a lot of money in it in one of them. He walked back to the men and kneeled down beside Bill. "Bill, how much money did you lose?"

Bill shook his head. "I'm not sure…maybe two thousand or so."

Tye took the money out of the bag and he and Wallace counted it. Wallace handed the money and the bag to Bill who took it with his left hand. "Looks you have a little over two thousand, boss." Bill nodded.

"Thanks, Wallace. Are you going after him?" he asked, looking at Tye.

Tye looked at Bill. "I'll bring him in. You stay at the fort till I return with the bastard." Tye made a travois for Bill, and

Wallace helped him lay the injured man on it. He gave Wallace and Lester directions to Clark, and started them on their way. They had the stolen horses as well as the dead men's horses. The horses should be no problem unless they encounter a storm and it spooks them.

Tye stepped into the saddle on Sandy, walked him to the river and let him drink his fill. Tye leaned down and filled both of his canteens. He always carried two, one for him and one for Sandy.

He led Sandy out of the river and nudged him into a trot following the tracks of Adam's horse. He gave a final wave to Wallace and Lester and then he was alone, and on the hunt again.

~~

Adam was excited and scared. After running his horse hard for a few minutes he begin to think clearer and common sense began to take over. He slowed his horse down to an easy canter. He was still shaking. He had never been shot at before and until that bastard Neuman killed Mrs. Ross and her son, he had never seen anyone killed.

"Dammit to hell," he thought. *"I should have seen what that bunch of shiftless bums were...thieves, killers, and drifters too lazy*

to work. How did I let them talk me into robbing Mr. Ross? That old man had always been good to me. Mrs. Ross…tears welled up in his eyes. He swallowed a lump in his throat. She was special…treated me just like one of the family. My God…how could I have been so stupid?" He beat his fist on his thigh several times. "*Stupid… just plain damn stupid."*

He looked over his shoulder and saw no one coming. He slowed his horse down to a walk. "*I've got to think straight,*" he thought. *"That's the only chance I have. What supplies do I have?"* He twisted in the saddle, opened his saddle bags and rummaged through them. He found a small package of coffee, a half dozen biscuits, a pound of jerky, and an extra shirt and a box of shells. He had the makings for smokes in his shirt pocket.

He laughed to himself. "*Here I am in the middle of nowhere; don't know where I am or where I'm going, very little food and one canteen of water. Besides all that good news, I probably have the best damn scout in the whole state after my ass."* He shook his head. *"You've got yourself in one hell of a fix and I don't see a way out. I had heard of Watkins, and if that dumb ass Neuman had not pulled his gun we might have bought a little time, and been a little more prepared to defend ourselves."* He looked down at his gun that rested on his thigh. "*Hell, I*

was so scared I never even pulled mine. I know the others fired some shots but I didn't." He looked up at the sky. *"God, if*

Second Chance

You will forgive me for what I was part of, I will never raise a hand against another man again."

He looked over his shoulder and seeing nothing, nudged his rested horse into a canter. He was headed north, keeping the Rio Grande about a mile to his left. He had no idea what was ahead of him, but he had a real good idea of what was behind him. He would need more supplies. He had a little cash, so if he stumbled onto a homestead he would buy what he needed.

~~

Tye came where the man had slowed his horse to a walk. Stepping down from the saddle he kneeled and traced the tracks with his finger. Judging from the tracks, he figured he was no more than an hour behind the killer. He stood up and looked around saying, "We might just end this before nightfall, Sandy." He stepped back into the saddle and kicked Sandy into a trot, glancing at the tracks every minute or so, but the rest of the time, he searched the hillsides for possible trouble. He suspected what the man was thinking and where he was going. Unless he was wrong, the man had few supplies.

The best bet to obtain them would be to stay close to the river, and seek out a homestead.

Gary McMillan

The terrain here was hills, arroyos, and brush. A half mile to the west, toward the river, the land was rocky with steep hills, cliffs, and little vegetation except for sage and cactus. He looked up at the position of the sun and figured it was an hour or so past noon. He glanced at the tracks and saw the man had nudged his horse into a canter. He did the same with Sandy and held the pace for twenty minutes before he reined to a halt. Dismounting, he took the extra canteen, pouring some water into his hat and gave Sandy a drink. While Sandy was sucking the water up, Tye surveyed the surrounding country. He looked at the sky. Dark clouds on the western horizon held a promise of rain, probably tonight. "That's all we need Sandy; cold and rain." He studied the clouds again. "*If it rains tracks will be hard to find tomorrow,*" he thought. "*I need to catch the bastard today.*"

He put away the canteen, put his hat on and shivered as a little water left in the hat ran down his collar. He mounted Sandy, nudging him into a canter. After four hours of alternating walking and trotting Sandy, he was no closer to the man. "*The man has a good horse,*" he thought. He slid from the saddle and kneeling, studied the tracks. "*I'm still about an hour behind him. The damn man not only has a good horse, but he knows how to get the most from him. There's no way I'm going to catch him tonight, so I might as well start looking for a place to camp that might offer a little shelter from the storm.*" He glanced at the sky and figured he had twenty or thirty minutes before the rain hit. The wind had picked up and Tye could smell rain.

Ten minutes later, as the wind whipped dust into the air, Tye found what he was looking for. To his left was a hill having a vertical cliff that looked fifteen or twenty feet high. If he could reach it, the cliff overhang would keep him fairly dry. He dismounted and led Sandy up the slope. When he reached the cliff, it was better than he had hoped. The first drop of rain began to fall as he picketed Sandy next to the wall of the cliff. The cliff ran almost due north and south, and with the wind and rain whistling in from the west, he should stay pretty dry. He laid his bedroll next to the cliff, and spread it out just as the rain hit in full force. Dry and warm under his blanket, he lay there watching the rain, thundering down in torrents one minute, but would let up to just a drizzle the next and then come down hard again. He rolled over on his side and went to sleep.

~~

Adam had his slicker on, but with the wind blowing, the rain was finding its way down his collar. He pulled his hat down low, and the slicker's collar tighter around his neck, and shivered. It was getting dark, and he knew he needed to find a place to ride the storm out. He should have stopped an hour earlier, but he was afraid to because Watkins was somewhere behind him.

His horse nickered, twitched its ears, and shook its head. Adam looked up and saw a homestead. "Thank you Lord," he mumbled. He entered the yard and shouted as loud as could, "HELLO THE HOUSE." The light went out immediately as the lamp was extinguished. A gun appeared at the window. The door opened.

"WHO'S THERE?" A man shouted.

"Adam Carter. I'm looking for a place to get out of this storm."

The lamp flared again and the door opened wide, although Adam saw that the gun in the window remained pointed straight at him. "Step down and come into the light," the voice said. Adam did as he was told. "Lift your hat so I can see your face." Adam did, and the man raised the lamp so the light illuminated a face that didn't look twenty years old. "Take off your pistol and hang it on the pommel of your saddle." Adam hesitated, and then did as he was told. "Hold your hands out to the side where I can see them and come on in."

Adam smiled, *this old man is careful enough,* he thought, *but maybe that's why he is still here.* He walked past the man and noticed a pistol in his right hand and the lamp in his left. The warmth hit him as soon as he walked through the door.

"Jacob, get your slicker on and take this man's horse to the barn and take its saddle off. Give him a little grain too." The young boy, about twelve or so, did as he was told. Adam glanced to the window and saw another young man holding the rifle on him. He was probably seventeen or eighteen. He had been the one holding the gun in the window.

"May I take my slicker off?" Adam asked. The man nodded and continued holding the pistol in his hand. Adam took off the slicker and walked to the door that was still open and shook it, getting most of the water off. He took off his hat and slapped it a couple times against the wall and put it back on his head. The man's wife smiled and handed him a cup of coffee.

"Adam..." the man paused. "That was your name wasn't it?"

"Yes sir."

"Well Adam, what in hell are you doing out on a night like this?"

Adam answered immediately. "My folks had a ranch several miles south of here. Two days ago while I was away working cattle, they were hit by Apaches. I heard the shooting, but by the time I got there the Indians had left, and my parents and our hand were dead." He hung his head and continued. "I buried my parents and Bill. Bill was our hired hand. The house was on fire, so I headed north. I'm looking to find Fort Clark. I'm thinking

56

about joining the army but I don't have a clue where I am or how to get there."

"George Wilson," the man said and stuck out his hand. When Adam took it, the man added, "That lady over there is my wife, Edith and that young man over there with the rifle is my oldest, James. Jacob is the one taking care of your horse."

"You don't know how much I appreciate you taking me in," Adam said. "I was pretty cold with all that water running down my collar." The lady came over and took his hand.

"Sit down here at the table and I'll fix you something to eat," she said. Adam sat down, the man sitting across from him. Adam noticed the young man named James still had the rifle in his hand. Mrs. Wilson sat a plate in front of him covered in fried potatoes and fried venison. He dug into the food and didn't look up until it was all gone. "Kinda hungry wasn't you," Mrs. Wilson said, laughing.

Embarrassed at how fast he had eaten. Adam said, "Guess so. It was mighty good Mrs. Wilson. Thank you." Jacob came back and said the horse was taken care of. "Mr. Wilson, do you mind if I sleep in the barn tonight?"

"You'll do no such thing young man," Mrs. Wilson said. "I will make you a pallet in front of the fire. That barn will be a might chilly on a night like this." Adam looked at Mr. Wilson and nodded his approval.

"I certainly appreciate the kindness. Mr. Wilson, can you give me directions to the fort?"

The man nodded. "Just keep going north till you hit the Old Mail Road. It will be only road out there. Head east on the road, the fort and the town of Brackettville is thirty or so miles."

"Sounds simple enough," Adam said. "I may be gone when you get up. I have a little cash with me. I would like to buy enough food for a couple days." Mrs. Wilson had the pallet made and spoke up.

You get to sleep. I'll set a sack of food on the table. You take it when you leave."

"Thank you, ma'am. You and your husband have been very kind." He walked over to the pallet, pulled off his boots and lay down on the blankets. "Goodnight."

"Goodnight to you, Adam," Mrs. Wilson said.

~~

Thin slivers of moonlight broke through the clouds as the storm passed. The sudden quietness woke Tye, and as usual when on scout or tracking someone, he lay motionless for a few seconds, listening for any signs of danger. It only took him a couple seconds to realize what had awakened him; the storm had passed. He sat up and looked at Sandy. Sandy was munching grass so he knew there was no one or anything close by. "That was quite a storm wasn't it boy?" Sandy nickered and Tye smiled. Both had remained, dry thanks to the overhang of the cliff.

Because of the clouds preventing him from seeing the stars, he wasn't sure what time it was. His pa had taught him to tell time by their positions at different times of the year. He had been tired when he lay down and he felt pretty good now, so he figured he must have slept for at least four or so hours which would make it about midnight. He lay back down, placed the palms of his hands under his head and stared at the sky. *"There's no sense in leaving before daylight. The rain surely had him holed up also and besides, the rain washed out all tracks he might have left. It will be a guessing game now as to where he is going."*

At times like this Tye fell back on things his pa had taught him, one of them being to put yourself in the man's place you are chasing and see what you would do. Supplies were the first thing that entered his mind.

"The only place he could find food would be homesteaders. The Mendehalls live a few miles north east of here, and the Wilson's live due north about five miles. He's not varied his direction one bit since he left the river, and the way he is going would take him to the Wilson's front door." With that thought, he shut his eyes and tried to go back to sleep.

Second Chance

~~

Adam woke, and lay there by the fireplace, the fire having burned down and only a few coals glowing like red eye balls in the darkness of the room. He sat up and placed a log on the coals. It was only a couple minutes before the log burst into flames and illuminated the room with its glow. He stood up and walked to the door and carefully opened it. The rain had stopped and he could see fairly well when the fast moving clouds allowed the light of the moon to shine through.

"*Watkins is probably taking advantage of the storm's passing and back on my trail. I probably would be smart to head out.*" He quietly shut the door and started to gather his things. "*Wait a minute,*" he thought. "*There's no tracks for him to follow because of the rain.*"

For the first time since leaving the river, he felt relaxed. There was no way Watkins could find any trace of my horse as hard as it rained. He sat down on the pallet, but not before noticing the sack of supplies on the table.

"*Mrs. Wilson did what she said. I must have been pretty tired and went to sleep quickly, because I don't remember her doing that.*"

He rummaged in his pocket and brought out a five dollar gold piece. He reached over and laid it on the table beside the sack. Lying back down, he sought a little more sleep.

Chapter Five

Adam was more than two miles from the Wilson's place when the first gray light of morning appeared over the eastern hills. The morning air was crisp with a fresh, clean smell after the rain. Adam felt better this morning because things were looking a little brighter. He had supplies for at least three days, and he figured that damn scout lost his tracks after the storm. Leaving money at the Wilson's for the supplies made him feel a little better about himself.

He wasn't sure where he was going as of yet. He had about thirty dollars on him so he figured if he came across another homestead he could buy some more supplies.

"I could keep on going north for a few days and then head east. I know there are some ranches up that way, and one may need a good hand. I might get lucky if I lay low and stay out of trouble. I had better change my name though, just in case someone asks questions about an Adam Carter."

He rode for a few minutes more trying to come up with a name to go by. He reined his horse in. Rolling the cigarette, he noticed his hands shaking a little, but figured it was the chill of the early morning. Sitting and watching his back trail, he smoked his cigarette.

"I always liked the name, James and I am young so I think I will become James Young." He laughed. *"That was easy enough,* he thought. He stroked his horse on the neck and shouted, "MY NAME IS JAMES YOUNG…DO YOU HEAR ME? JAMES YOUNG IS MY NAME." His horse looked back at him and shook his head. Smiling, Adam reined his horse around and galloped north.

~

Tye was trotting Sandy, heading for the closest homestead he knew of, the Wilson's. Adams tracks were gone, thanks to the rain, so he was playing a hunch that he had found shelter at the Wilson's and that bothered him. He was afraid of what the man might do if the Wilson's got too nosey and asked the wrong questions. He was still a ways from the homestead and was going to be too late to help if they had. He had known George and Edith Wilson for a couple of years. He knew they had a couple of sons, one about fifteen or so, and one ten or eleven, but couldn't remember their names. They seem like good people and like most others settling out here, just wanted to be left alone to live their lives.

Worrying something might have happened he nudged Sandy into an easy gallop. Twenty minutes later, he was relieved to see smoke coming from the chimney of the house. Two horses were in the corral and chickens were scurrying about. Everything looked normal, so he rode Sandy down the hill and into the yard.

The door opened and a deep voice boomed from inside the house, "Tye Watkins, what are you doing here?" George walked out holding his pistol in his right hand, but quickly shifted it to his left and extended his right to Tye. Tye, who had noticed the barrel of the rifle pointed at him from the window as he rode up, dismounted and took the man's hand.

"Tracking a man who killed a rancher's wife and son," Tye answered.

George looked at his wife who had come out. "How are you Tye?" she asked.

Tye took off his hat. "Good to see you Mrs. Wilson."

George asked. "Who is this man so we can be on the look out for him?"

"A young man, maybe twenty-one give or take a year. His name is Adam Carter."

Mrs. Wilson put her hand to her mouth, a look of disbelief on her face. George put his arm around her shoulders and hugged her to his chest. "Are you sure this is the man you are after."

Tye knew immediately they had seen him. "I only know he is young and his name. I could not identify him if I had to. I can identify his horse though. His left rear hoof has a notch in the shoe. I take it he came by?"

"More than that, Tye. We fed him and he slept here," he said pointing to the area in front of the fireplace. "We left him some food on the table and he left a five dollar gold piece when he left."

"He left money?" Tye asked. This surprised him. "What time did he leave?"

"He was gone when we got up," Mrs. Wilson answered. "I can't believe that nice young man is a killer. Why, he told us his parents were killed on a ranch south of here two days ago."

Tye, holding his hat in front of him and nervously fingering the brim replied. The man I am chasing worked on a ranch southwest of San Antonio. Five days ago, he and four friends killed the wife and fifteen year old son of the rancher who owned the Rocking B Ranch. The rancher, two of his men and me, caught up with them when they were crossing into Mexico south of here. The others were killed and the rancher and one of his men were wounded. They are on their way to Fort Clark to see the post surgeon. I have been chasing Adam since, but lost his tracks last night in the storm."

"It was him," a young man said as he came from the house.

"Tye, this is our son, Jacob," George said. Tye shook the young man's hand.

"How do you know it was the man I'm chasing?" Tye asked.

"His horse had a B brand on it and under it was a curved line."

"Like the bottom of a rocking chair?" Tye asked. The boy nodded.

Tye looked at George. "Did he say where he was going?"

"Fort Clark to join the army," Mrs. Wilson said before George could answer.

George looked at her and nodded. "I figure that was also a lie."

"That's okay. His tracks won't be hard to follow, and I'm wasting time. He tipped his hat to Mrs. Wilson and shook George's hand. He mounted Sandy. "In the future George, ya'll be a little more careful who let in your home." He reined Sandy around and rode out of the yard and headed north, following the tracks of the horse with the Rocking B brand. He figured he was at least three hours behind the killer. As he rode he had some troubling thoughts about this man.

"This is the strangest man I ever hunted. If he really is a cold blooded killer, why did he leave the Wilson's alive knowing I was behind him and would be talking to them? Why did he leave

money? That's not like a thief. How come at the crossing he didn't fight? His gun could have made a difference and as far as I know, he never fired a shot. He could have had a few more hours' head start if he had left when the storm passed, but he obviously waited a couple hours."

Tye kicked Sandy into a gallop and figured when he caught up with this man all his questions would be answered.

～～

James Young, formerly Adam Carter, rode up to the Old San Diego/San Antonio Mail Road about noon. He sat on his horse in the middle of the road, pondering what to do. Going right would lead him to Fort Clark and Brackettville. Going left would lead him he didn't know where for sure. He wanted to keep headed north but he also could use a drink and he figured there were saloons in Brackettville, so he headed that way.

～～

Bill Ross lay in the post hospital bed, his wound cleaned and bandaged. His employees, Lester and Wallace were in the room visiting him. Wallace had brought both in last night just before the storm struck, which had been fortunate because in their condition, getting soaked and cold would probably led to pneumonia.

"I wonder if Tye has caught that bastard, Carter?" Bill asked.

"We haven't heard a word, boss. If he hasn't, I hope he didn't lose the trail after that damn storm last night," Wallace answered.

"How's the shoulder, Lester?" Bill asked.

"About like yours, I imagine," he said. "Only hurts when my heart beats."

"I know the feeling," Bill said smiling, and then grimaced as a new wave of pain racked him. "Damn, I need some whiskey," he mumbled.

"What you need is some sleep, so we are leaving. We'll see you later," Lester said as they left.

~~

The sun was low in the west when Adam rode into Brackettville, stopping at the first saloon he saw. Entering, he headed straight to the bar and ordered whiskey. He quickly downed it, and took the bottle to a table against the back wall. Only two tables were occupied, one had three men and the other had two. The saloon was typical; dimly lit except in the center. It smelled of tobacco and the odor of unwashed bodies. The wall behind the bar featured a large nude painting of a woman. The bartender said his name was Jim and said since he didn't recognize me, I must first time customer. He said the first drink was on him. Adam refilled his glass and sipped it this time, taking his time feeling the warmth that flowed through his body. One of the girls came over, but he waved her away. His plan was to finish off the bottle, and leave.

At the O'Malley's home across the road from Brackettville at Fort Clark, Sergeant O'Malley was telling his wife, Rebecca and Buff, who were over for supper, the most amazing thing he had ever seen. He nodded at Todd, eating at another table. "Todd and I were over at the stables this afternoon to watch Jacobson, our wrangler, break some horses. He had this one horse, a beautiful sorrel, who was giving him a hard time. Jacobson had a coil of rope in his hand, and struck the horse across the forelock with it. Before I could say anything, young Todd climbed through the fence, and ran to where Jacobson and the horse were. He shoved the man aside, and grabbed the rope that was around the horse's neck. Then he began to talk to the excited animal. Almost immediately, the horse calmed down, and did not move as Todd eased up next to the sorrel and scratched the horse under the lower jaw."

Second Chance

"Jacobson gave me a dumfounded look. I tell you, I never saw anything like it. The boy rubbed that horse and the animal never moved-never twitched a muscle. As Jacobson and I watched, Todd led the horse next to the fence. He stepped on the bottom rail and slowly eased himself onto the sorrel's back. He leaned forward and scratched both sides of the animal's neck. This wild horse never moved. It did not even nicker. After a couple minutes, Todd sat upright and nudged the horse's flanks with his heels. The horse started walking and Todd rode him around the corral."

"After about five minutes he slid off the horse and stood in front of the sorrel and I'll be damned if that animal didn't lower his head so the boy could scratch him between the ears. Todd picked the blanket off the fence, and held it in front of the animal's nose. He then stepped to the side, and gently laid the blanket on the horse's back. He waited a moment, picked up the saddle and laid it on the blanket. He bent down and reaching under the horse's belly, tightened the girth. He stepped in front of the horse, and actually had the horse's head resting on his shoulder as he scratched both sides of the horse's neck. Jacobson asked who in hell that kid was. I just laughed and said he lives with me, but I don't know much about him. I told him Todd's story while we watched Todd step into the saddle. The horse bucked a couple times, and then settled down, and Todd rode him around the stables for several minutes. He finally dismounted, and walked

70

away from the horse to the far side of the corral. I kid you not, that horse followed him and actually nudged him with his nose a couple of times. He took the reins and walking the horse over to where we were standing, handed the reins to the old wrangler. Todd started to walk away, but turned back." O'Malley chuckled. "You're not going to believe what that boy said to old Jacobson." O'Malley laughed again so hard his shoulders were shaking. "Todd looked straight at Jacobson and said, 'Sir, your job would be a lot easier if you knew something about horses.'"

"I would have given anything for ya'll to have seen the look on the wrangler's face. He had a reputation as a rough and tough top notch hand when it came to breaking horses but was also known to be a little cruel. The man was dumfounded; didn't know what to say. Only time I had ever been around him that his mouth wasn't working and it got shut up by a fourteen year old boy." He turned around in the chair and tousled Todd's hair and smiled. "This here boy was something else out there today."

Rebecca asked Todd. "Have you done that before?"

"I've always had a way with animals, especially horses. I knew I shouldn't have done what I did today, but I just don't like to see animals mistreated."

Buff spoke up. "I saw a man one time in the mountains that had a special talent like that. He could take the meanest, stubbornness, old mule you ever saw, and sweet talk that animal into eating out of his hand if he wanted. I saw him do it more than once too." He chuckled, "Tye will get a kick out of that story about Todd."

Chapter Six

Tye followed the tracks of the outlaw to the Old Mail Road. Due to the number of tracks of people traveling the road since the rain, it took him a while to find the ones he was looking for. The fact the man was headed where he was, surprised Tye.

"Why would a man on the run head for a town instead of across the border where no one would know him? If nothing else, I would have kept going north. There's a hell of a lot of open country there where a man could disappear. The last damn place I would go would be a town with a fort just across the road with a couple hundred soldiers where I might just be recognized. A smart man on the run tries to leave as little a hint regarding where he is going as possible."

In the end, Tye didn't know whether this was the dumbest man he has ever chased or just the most careless. Tye headed toward Brackettville, but wasn't sure the man would go all the way into town. As he rode, he kept an eye on the wet ground north of the road for tracks. When darkness settled in around him, and it became impossible to see tracks on the ground, he decided to take the gamble that the man went to Brackettville. He was still an hour from town, so he nudged Sandy into an easy gallop.

Second Chance

~~

The man sitting at the table against the back wall could not be seen clearly since the light from the kerosene lamp hanging in the center of the room had his table in the shadows. That is the reason he had chosen the table, plus the fact his back was against the wall. Adam had just drained the last drop in his glass, and as he poured himself another two men walked in, each getting his immediate attention. Wallace Anderson and Lester Hindman, his former co-workers on the Rocking B Ranch, entered the saloon.

Adam immediately pulled his hat down low. The two men paid no attention to anyone as they headed straight for the bar. Adam raised his head just enough to watch them from under the brim of his hat. They stood at the bar. Lester had his arm in a sling.

"I wonder if Mr. Ross was hit also. I bet he was, and they brought him here to receive medical help. They've bought a bottle so they are going to be here for awhile. He watched them for a few minutes as they spoke with the barkeep. They're going to look around sooner or later, so somehow, I've got to get out of here.

Looking around while keeping his head down, to his left maybe ten feet was a door he figured led outside to the outhouse. He stuck the cork back in the bottle and slid the bottle inside his shirt. He sipped the rest of his drink, and cursed himself for being so stupid in coming here. He was just scooting his chair back to get up when two soldiers walked in. He sat back down.

The two soldiers walked over to the bar and stood next to Wallace and Lester. One of the soldiers, a sergeant asked. "You the two ranch hands that brought the rancher in?"

Wallace answered. "Yeah, we brought him in. I'm Wallace Anderson and this old codger next to me is Lester Hindman." He held out his hand and the sergeant took it. "This here is Corporal Absher and I'm Arnold." After shaking hands, Sergeant Arnold asked about the gun fight and the man Tye was after.

Wallace spoke. "Thanks to Tye, we got to the crossing ahead of them and hid in the brush along the hillside while Tye went down to check for tracks. They showed up while he was down there and things went to hell quick. Bullets were flying everywhere. Lester here took one in the shoulder, and Mr. Ross got hit hard. All the outlaws were down, except the one we wanted most, Adam Carter. He had run off like a scared rabbit. Carter worked with us on the Rocking B, and Mr. Ross and his wife had treated him like family, just like they do us. Mr. Ross was hurt deep by the fact that bastard turned against him and killed his wife and son. He wants him dead."

Adam swallowed hard, beads of sweat trailing slowly down his face and dripping on the wooden table.

Arnold spoke. "I can tolerate, even understand some men who rob and sometimes someone is accidentally killed, but not turning on someone who gave you a job and treats you like you said they did. A man like that deserves anything he gets, and I guarantee you Tye will find him. I've been here at Fort Clark for two years now and not a single time as Tye not come in with the man he was sent after. Sometimes, they were a little worse for wear like that Yancey Cates fellow or sometimes just plain dead," he said chuckling.

"Who was the Cates fellow?" Wallace asked.

Arnold slammed his glass down on the bar, spilling his drink startling the two ranch hands. "I'll tell you who the hell he was. Yancey and his brother Billy were ex-Confederate soldiers as were the members of their gang. They hated us bluecoats and would shoot at one on sight. The killed a couple soldiers who were good friends of mine. They also killed several homesteaders; men, women, and even children. They done things to some of those good people that you would not believe. Tye tracked them down, and eventually he and the soldiers with him killed them all except for Yancey. Well, Yancey thought himself to be pretty tough, so he started in on Tye and the Army, calling them every vile name he could think of. Tye ignored him until he started in on Tye's wife.

Tye had one of the soldiers untie the man and Tye whipped him like you ain't ever seen a man get whipped. He didn't talk much after that."

Lester put down his glass and spoke. "I've heard of this man you are talking about, Tye Watkins. Wallace rode with him and his father while he was with the Rangers. I guess ya'll know him pretty well?"

Corporal Absher laughed. "You could say that. There's not a soldier or officer at Fort Clark that hasn't had his ass saved at least once by that man. He's the meanest, toughest man that ever forked a horse. Hell, even the Apaches are afraid of him, and as you know, they fear nothing."

Arnold butted in. "Tye is as much Apache as the Apache is. He can live off the land like they do, he can track better than most of them, and he is hell on earth in a fight whether it is with knives, tomahawks, guns, or fists. When he gets on a man's trail, it's just a matter of time before he finds him. Hell, when he was with the Texas Long Rifles, or as some people called them Rangers, he tracked so many bandits down a bounty was placed on him. He's still here, and he hates men who prey on homesteaders. Your friend is as good as dead."

Wallace slammed his glass on the bar. "The bastard is no friend of ours! I hope that damn scout catches him and skins that piece of horse dun alive."

Adam could take no more. He slid the chair back, took three quick steps, opened the door and stepped outside. He listened for a moment to see if anyone was coming across the wooden floor, but heard no sounds. He walked past a couple of buildings and turned left to find his horse. Mounting, he rode to the back of the building before getting back on the road and heading out of town. *"Lester and Wallace must have had a lot on their minds not to have noticed my horse with the Rocking B brand on it outside the saloon."* He was thankful for that.

He was scared-scared like he had never been before. He figured what those soldiers said was true, because he had heard some pretty wild stories about this scout. He figured he was as good as dead. He slipped the bottle out of his shirt and took a long drink. He could not believe he had been so stupid as to enter this two bit town to get a drink, and come within a hair of being recognized.

Something white ahead of him in the road got his attention. It was a couple of seconds before he realized what it was. A large herd of goats was crossing the road when a thought struck him.

"The goats might just cover my tracks if I leave the road. If that scout is as good as they say, he will be back on my trail, but it won't be till daylight and daylight is hours away. I'll be in the hill country by then.

He headed north, remaining in the middle of the goat's tracks, feeling better about the situation he had gotten himself into.

~~

Tye arrived in Brackettville about nine that night, and stopped at the first saloon. After entering, he was surprised to see Wallace and Lester sitting at a table.

"What the hell!" Wallace exclaimed! "Where's Adam?"

"Sit down Wallace," Tye said, taking a chair. "I'm about two hours behind him, and I figure he came through here about dark." He turned to the bar keep. "Jim, can you come over here for a second?" He had known the barkeep for a couple of years, and he would tell him if a stranger had stopped by. "Jim has any strangers been by tonight?" he asked.

Bill shrugged his shoulders and said, "Only that cowboy at the back table." They all looked at the same time.

"What cowboy," Lester asked?

"I don't know where he went," Jim said. "He came in about a half hour before you two. He bought a bottle and sat at that back table. I never paid him any more attention."

Tye knowing all barkeeps had an eye for detail and gossip asked, "What did this cowboy look like?"

"Hell, just like all cowboys. He was young, maybe twenty or so, and I guess he could be considered a little over average height and weighing one hundred fifty or so pounds. He had a light blue shirt that was dirty as hell, a brown leather vest, and brown pants. He wore a pistol on his right hip and a yellow kerchief." He thought for a minute. "Oh yeah, he had blonde hair that touched his collar in back."

"SONOFABITCH," Wallace said slamming his fist on the table. The bastard was right behind us Lester, and we didn't see him."

"Calm down, Wallace. Just calm the hell down," Tye said calmly. "He took that seat back there for a reason. Take another look. If he had been there, you probably would not have recognized him in the shadows. He's not as careless as I thought." Tye filled them in on the chase so far including him leaving money at the Wilson's. "What can you tell me about him?"

"He's a top hand," Lester responded, his good right hand resting on Wallace's shoulder trying to calm his friend down. "Good worker and always been dependable. He was there over a year, and never any trouble. He would go to San Antonio the weekend he got paid, and would always come back like all cowboys do...broke. Wallace and me liked him...we all got along well."

"Do you know anything about his past?"

"He never said anything about it," a calmer Wallace answered. "You know how it is with cowboys, one doesn't ask questions about another's past. A cowboy is judged by what he is now, and as long as he is loyal to the brand and does his job, no one is really interested in what he might have done in the past."

Tye nodded his head. He knew that most men in this country didn't care about a person's past, and it was considered rude to ask. If a man wanted you to know something, he would tell you. Riding for the brand, which meant being loyal to the rancher he worked for, was the way a cowboy was judged by other cowboys. He could relate to that idea with the soldiers he scouted for here at Clark. He suspected some of the best soldiers here at the fort probably had a shadowy past. When push came to shove, all that mattered was dependability.

"Are you going after him?" Wallace asked.

Tye was a little agitated at his question. "Hell yes I'm going after him," he said, a touch of anger in his voice, "But not tonight. There is no way I can follow his tracks in the dark. This rain we had covered a wide area so he's going to leave tracks. I'll pick them up in the morning." He stood up. "I'll see you when I bring him back." He walked out of the saloon, mounted Sandy, and rode across the bridge over Los Moras Creek and into Fort Clark. He headed directly to Post Headquarters to see if maybe Thurston was still there before going to see Rebecca.

"Evening Tye," the guard said as he crossed the bridge.

Tye didn't know the soldier's name, but recognized him from some of the patrols he was on that Tye was scouting for. "Evening to you too," Tye said leaning down and shaking the man's hand. "Have a pleasant evening," Tye said and continued toward the headquarters building. He could see a light on and figured Thurston was there. It seemed like he was always there. His wife had left him shortly after he took over as Post Commander. She had come from a rich family back east, and just never adapted to the type of life out here where there weren't dances every night and fancy restaurants to frequent. The major's whole life now centered on his job at Fort Clark, and he had done a great job as far as Tye was concerned.

Just as Tye stepped down from Sandy in front of headquarters, Major Thurston stepped out on the porch.

"TYE!" he said, surprise written across his face. "What are you doing here?"

"It's a long story, Tye said, shaking Thurston's hand.

"Have a seat beside me," Thurston said, sitting down on the top step of the wooden porch.

Thurston lit a cigar and took a quick couple of puffs. "I'm waiting," he said and offered Tye a cigar. Tye started from the beginning when he met Ross and filled him in on everything up to the saloon.

"I can't figure this man out, Major."

"What do you mean by that?"

"He supposedly robbed Ross and killed the man's wife and son, yet he did not fire on me or the Rocking B men at the crossing. He had every opportunity to rob and possibly kill the Wilson's but didn't, and on top of that, he left five dollars for the food they were giving to him free."

"I see what you mean. Could be he got talked into this thing at the Rocking B and the situation got out of hand. Maybe he didn't kill those people."

"That's just about what I've decided. I think those other men did exactly what you said, talked him into this mess and they did the killing. The man at the crossing that I talked to had that look I've seen a hundred times in a man that could kill you without a second thought. He had those eyes that I call dead man eyes, crazy, cold, no feeling. He knew he had guns aimed at him, he knew he was probably going to die, but he drew anyway." Tye shook his head. "It takes all kinds I guess."

"What are you going to do?

"I'll leave at daybreak, try to pick up his trail, and hopefully find him."

"Then what?"

"I'll bring him to you and let you decide. My job is, as my pa use to say, bring them in and don't judge them. That's for courts and God to do."

Thurston laughed. "You pa was a wise man. Anyway, normally in a case like this, he would go to a regular court to be tried unless he breaks a law on the fort or harms a soldier, but since there is no court and no law around here, I could make a decision as to his fate." Nothing was said for a moment as he puffed on his cigar a couple times. "There was a report of Apache trouble northwest of here. A couple of men came by and told me. I sent a patrol out this morning led by Captain McClellan. Dan is scouting for him."

"Dan will do a good job for the captain."

Thurston just grunted. "I wish you had been here. I know Dan is good, but he's not you." He stood up. "You need to see that little wife of yours, so get going. I'll have some supplies ready when you leave. Leave Sandy, and I'll have him taken to the stables and fed."

Tye stood up and shook the major's hand. "I'll see you in a couple of days or so."

Thurston nodded and they parted. Thurston stopped after a dozen steps or so and turned back, hollering at Tye.

"Be sure you ask Buff about that Jenkins boy," and he laughed loud enough for Tye to hear him.

"What about the boy?"

"I'll let Buff tell you. Goodnight." Tye stood there watching the major disappear, wondering what was going on. He started to ask again, but decided against it. He would ask Buff about Todd. Tye walked home. He knew Buff took his responsibility as Rebecca's protector seriously when he was away, and didn't want to get shot by barging in the door unannounced. He stepped on the porch.

"Buff, it's Tye. I'm coming in." He heard a chair scraping on the floor. The door swung open, and Buff stood there, a look of surprise on his face.

"Tye!" Buff exclaimed. "What in the world are you doing here?"

"I live here, you old coot," Tye said, laughing and hugging the old trapper. Buff patted him vigorously on the back.

"Buff, what's going on out there?" Rebecca asked from the bedroom. Tye put his finger on his lips signaling Buff to be quiet. Tye walked to the bedroom door, quickly opened it and stepped in.

"Is there room in that bed for a smelly old scout?"

"Tye...Tye," she said throwing the covers back and moving toward him. They embraced each other and showered each other with kisses. After a moment he pushed her back away and looked down at her stomach. He dropped to his knees and pulled her stomach against his face. She stood still, her fingers in his hair, as he turned his head and put his ear against her stomach and listened. After a moment he jerked his head away.

"The little thing just kicked me," he said excitedly. "I felt him kick me."

"May be a her," Rebecca said.

"Whatever. I don't care," he said, standing up and hugging her again. "I love you, Rebecca."

She kissed him. "I love you Tye…more than anything in the world." She stepped back away from him. "What are you doing here? Did you catch the man? How long can you stay?"

Tye waved his hands in front of him. "Hold on just a minute. One question at a time, honey." They both laughed. Rebecca put her robe on and they walked into the main room where Buff was standing, a big smile across his face. They sat down at the table and Tye filled them in on the chase, saying he would be leaving about daylight in the morning.

"It takes a pretty sorry human to kill someone who has given them work and a place to live," Buff said.

"It does, Buff, but I'm not sure about this guy. He's different than any man I have chased before. I told you he spent the night with some people I know, the Wilson's. They told me how polite he was, and they provided food for him to take when he left. He put five dollars on the table when he left. Does that sound like an outlaw? At the saloon awhile ago, the two men he worked with were shocked he had been part of this mess. They liked him, said he was a good hand and never a problem. To me, he does not fit the mold of a killer and thief."

"I see what you mean," Buff replied.

"Do you really think he killed those people?" Rebecca asked.

"No, I don't. I know he was there which makes him guilty, but as far as being part of the actual killing, I don't think so. I'm hoping to bring him in alive, and let Thurston decide." He looked at Rebecca. "Let's change the subject for a second. How are you?"

Rebecca smiled, "I'm fine. The doctor said about two or three weeks." Tye put his sun-darken hand on her small delicate hand and gave it a gentle squeeze.

"That's great, honey." He leaned over and kissed her on the cheek. "Now, the second thing I want to know. What's the deal with Todd? The major said you would tell me something about him I should know," he said, looking at Buff.

Buff leaned back in his chair. "Tye, that boy has a special talent." He commenced to tell Tye the events of that afternoon at the stables as related to them by Sergeant O'Malley. Tye sat dumfounded.

"I've never heard such a story. That's the most remarkable thing I have ever heard."

"I told O'Malley I saw a man back in the mountains that could do that with mules and you know how mean and stubborn they can be," Buff said.

Tye nodded. "After spending as much time as I have with him lately, it really shouldn't shock me." Tye looked away as if letting the story sink in. "I knew there was something different about that kid from the very first time he was around Sandy. That horse is sort of particular about who gets close to him. I watched Todd walk right up and scratch him on the neck. Sandy didn't even twitch. I'll be anxious to talk to him when I get back."

"When will that be?" Rebecca asked squeezing his arm.

"I don't know for sure, honey. Maybe in a day, may be three or four…ever how long it takes me to find the man and bring him back."

Buff asked. "Did Thurston say anything about the Apache trouble?"

Tye nodded. "He said he had Dan scouting for a patrol led by McClellan."

"Do you think there is anything to it?"

"We haven't had any trouble for awhile, but there's always a young, hot headed buck out there wanting to live the way his father did. To answer your question…yes, there is a good probability the story is true."

"May I say something?" Rebecca asked.

"Say anything you want," Tye replied.

"If you are coming to bed with me you are gong to take a bath," she said holding her nose. "You smell worse than a sweaty horse." She laughed and closed the door.

Tye looked at the closed door and then at Buff. "I guess I had better heat some water and do like she says."

"You do that." Buff laughed. "You do smell a little ripe. As for me, I'm going to bed." Buff chuckled again and walked into his room.

Tye placed a couple pieces of stove wood on the hot coals. The wood flared up in a couple of minutes, and Tye placed a bucket of water on to heat. He walked to the creek with two other buckets and filled them. Back inside the house, he poured them into the tub, stripped his clothes, and waited for a couple minutes for the water to get hot. When the water commenced boiling, he poured it into the tub, tested it, and then eased himself into the warm water.

Chapter Seven

Tye was on the Old Mail Road as the first rays of the morning sun touched the damp landscape east of Brackettville. Tye was again searching the ground for any fresh tracks leaving the road and heading north. The air was crisp and the rays of the sun felt good as he nudged Sandy into a trot. Tracks would be easily seen in the damp ground, so he felt confident that at even a trot, he would recognize them. His looking for Adam's horse tracks along this part of the road between Brackettville and Fort Inge reminded him of an earlier chase he had; a chase where he was trying to catch Yancey Cates. Yancey was a very vicious man. Tye had captured him earlier after killing Yancey's brother and all the gang members. Later, Yancey escaped with the help of friends. He had sworn he was going to kill Tye's wife, Rebecca, for the scout's part in the demise of his gang, and especially for his brother's death. It had been a frantic chase, but Rebecca was alive and well and Yancey…well, he had the hell beat out of him again by Tye and then later, he met the hangman.

After about an hour of searching, Tye encountered the tracks of the goat herd. Curious, he stepped down from Sandy and kneeled for a closer look. After a minute of close inspection, Tye smiled.

"*Good try Mr. Carter,*" he thought to himself, "*but you aren't the first to try that old trick.*" Tye stood up and stared at the low hills that were visible to the north; the same hills he had chased Yancey through. As far as he could see after mounting Sandy, the goat tracks were clearly visible. Tye knew the man would leave the tracks sooner or later. He could not see both sides to see the tracks of the horse leaving because the goat tracks were over an area about thirty yards wide. He mumbled a curse under his breath because of the size of the herd. He sat there a few minutes pondering which side of the tracks to follow.

"*If I was him, I would stay in them for as long as possible. East or west…that is the question? If I'm a cowboy, which direction offers the best chance of losing myself by working on a big ranch. West are mostly homesteaders and land not fit to feed large herds of cattle. East was the best choice since the land was suitable for cattle…at least that is what he had been told. Fort McKavett lay in that direction. The fort was home of the 24th and 25th infantry along with the 9th and 10th Calvary. The troops were black Americans and formed what was fondly called the Buffalo Soldiers. That was the name given them by the Comanche because of their black skin and curly hair. If need be, I might get some help there.*"

Second Chance

He reined Sandy in just outside of the goat tracks on the east side and headed north watching for tracks leaving. Thirty minutes later he halted Sandy. He had the feeling he was not alone. Being who he was and what he did, he trusted his senses and they had saved him more than once. He searched the area ahead and both sides, but saw nothing. He twisted in the saddle and looked back. A man was dogging his trail. Tye took his Henry out of the saddle scabbard, laid it across his thighs, reined Sandy around to face the man and waited.

~~

Adam sat on his horse, a cigarette dangling from his lips, looking at the landscape ahead of him. He had left the goat tracks hours ago as he angled to the northeast. He had seen no sign of any homes, ranches, or roads. He sat there pondering which way to go.

As he sat there, he was startled to hear what sounded like a cow bellowing. He rode in the direction the sound came from. After about a hundred yards he pulled up and listened. He could hear the sounds clearly now, and knew it was cattle, and a lot of them. He nudged his horse into a trot, the sounds becoming louder with each step of his horse. Upon topping a low hill, a smile spread across his face. A large herd of cattle was grazing in the little valley below. Two cowboys watched them. As he watched, one of the men pointed toward where he was sitting on the hill. The other man rode over and also looked at Adam.

Adam eased his horse down the fairly steep slope toward the men. As he rode, he watched both pull their rifles out and lay them across their saddles. When he was fifty yards away, he held both hands out to his side and guided his horse with his knees. The horse was used to working cattle, and with Adam using both hands for roping, he was used to responding to the pressure from his masters knees.

Adam stopped twenty yards from the two cowboys.

"Who are you, and what do you want?" the larger of the two men asked. Adam noticed both men had the barrels of their rifles pointed in his general direction. Adam noted the rifles because he had done the same thing when strangers approached him while he was working cattle at the Rocking B.

"James Young," Adam replied to the question. "I'm looking for work."

The two men kicked their horses and came to him, one on each side. Adam lowered his hands and rested them on the pommel of his saddle.

"You two would make me feel a hell of lot better if you would point those rifles in another direction," James said with a grin on his face. "I'm just an out of work cowboy looking to find a place to throw my bedroll."

The big man looked him over. "Let me see one of your hands." Adam stuck out his hand and the man took it with his left, his right still on the trigger of the Henry repeater. Adam noticed the barrel was still pointed at his belly. He turned Adam's hand over and looked at the palm. He saw the hardened skin from a lot of hard work, and that one finger had been broken and not set right. "What happened to your finger?"

"Got it caught between the rope and pommel with a damn steer on the other end."

The big man nodded. "Saw a fellow lose a finger like that once. Where did you say you worked?"

Adam relaxed a little as he saw the barrel of the Henry move ever so slightly away from the direction of his belly.

"Didn't say, but I rode for the Lazy S brand down south about a hundred and fifty miles until a week ago and before that, the Double D close to San Antonio." He looked at the big man. "Your boss hiring?"

"Nope the other, smaller man said. He ain't hiring drifters today."

Adam raised his butt up off the saddle and then settled back down and leaned toward the man who just spoke. "I am not no drifter, mister. I'm a cowhand looking for work and will give an honest days work for his pay," he replied rather sternly.

The big man spoke. "The ranch is about a mile up this canyon. The man's name is Lucas Riley. Go see him and tell him Bill Riley sent you."

Adam noticed the last name. "Kin to him?"

The man named Bill nodded. "He's my pa." Adam nodded and rode away toward the ranch.

The smaller man looked at Bill. "Shouldn't one of us watch him?"

"Naw. I could tell by his hands and the way he rode that horse he's a cowhand." He turned and watched Adam disappear up the canyon. "Just an out-of-work cowboy."

~~

The rider approaching Tye was less than fifty yards away before Tye recognized him. He put the Henry in its scabbard and waited prior to speaking.

"Wallace, what in hell are you doing out here?"

Wallace grinned. "Thought maybe that old cowboy would be too tough for you so I came to help out." Both men laughed, and shook hands.

"I started to ask you if you wanted to come along when we were talking in the saloon last night."

Wallace shrugged his shoulders. "I probably would have said no, but I got to thinking about everything; you know, Bill shot and in bad shape, and Lester with the shoulder wound. I decided about daylight I wanted to have a hand in bringing Adam in. Besides, you don't know what he looks like, and could be talking to the sonofabitch and not even know it."

Tye thought about that for a moment and knew it was a good point. "Glad to have you along, but remember, I want him alive if at all possible." Wallace nodded.

"I want him alive too. Shooting him would be too quick. I want to see him sweat; waiting to be hung."

Tye started to say something about his feeling toward the outlaw but decided against it. He would probably be wasting his time because Wallace was full of hate right now for the man and would not listen. "How did you find me anyway?"

"Remember I was with the Rangers when you and your pa were with them. I did some tracking. It's something you don't forget. I followed your horse's tracks to where the goats crossed the road and they did not come out one the other side, so I took a close look and found them headed north, staying just outside of the goats tracks. I figured you were looking for tracks leaving on the east side, so I rode on the west side. He didn't leave that way."

Tye was impressed with this man. He studied him for a moment: he was of medium build, maybe forty or forty-five years old, his hair was as black as a raven's, no gray. His face was covered by a beard needing trimming. Both dark eyes were hooded with protruding, heavy eyebrows. Tye nodded to the man.

"Let's head north and see if we can find him. You stay on the west side and watch for any tracks leaving the goat trail." Wallace grunted and led his horse to the other side.

~~

From his horse, Adam stared at a ranch house about two hundred yards in front of him. It was huge compared to others he had seen. A man could put two of the Rocking B headquarters inside with room left over. A two-story barn could be seen with a corral behind it. He could see a dozen horses, and assumed there were more behind the barn. A bunkhouse on the opposite side of the house looked large enough for a dozen men to sleep there.

He nudged his horse forward, and as he neared the ranch house he became more impressed. The place was immaculate, and built to last forever. A shaded porch ran the entire length of the rocky front of the house; chimneys protruded from each end of the roof. The roof was probably wood but had several inches of dirt on top serving two purposes; to keep the heat from the sun out in summer and the heat in during the winter and second, it would be difficult for the Indians or anyone else to burn it down.

"This is one hell of a spread", he thought to himself.

He sat on his horse and shouted, "HELLO THE HOUSE." It seemed like a minute passed before the door opened, but actually was only a few seconds. The prettiest girl he had ever seen stepped out, followed by the biggest man he had ever seen.

"Step down," the big man said, "And tell me what I can do for you."

Adam swung his leg over, and just before his right foot hit the ground, he saw the rifle pointed at him from one of the windows. "I don't mean no harm mister and I would appreciate your asking who ever has that rifle pointed at me to lower it some. It makes a man nervous knowing an accidental twitch of a finger could cause him some pain."

The big man smiled as he signaled for the gun to be lowered. "If it went off, it would be no accident. That woman of mine has killed her share of raiding Comanche, and a couple of no good white men that meant her harm. Now come over here to the porch and have a seat." Adam stepped onto the porch, took a chair and sat down next to the girl. He got a whiff of perfume and then remembered it had been days since he had bathed and he probably smelled like a horse. He hoped what little breeze there was kept his odor away from her.

"I take it you're Mr. Riley?" Adam asked.

The big man looked at him a little closer. "How did you know my name?"

"I met your son, Bill, a ways back. He gave me directions to the house."

"Why would he do that?"

"I'm looking for work. I thought maybe you could use a top hand."

"You look a little young to be…as you say, a top hand," Riley said, as the corners of his mouth curled up in a slight smile.

"I've been working cattle since I was fifteen or sixteen."

"And just how old are you now Mr.…." the girl hesitated, and then added. "What is your name anyway?"

"James Young, Ma'am."

"Well then Mr. Young, exactly how old are you?" she asked.

"Twenty-three, Ma'am…be twenty-four next month." Her interest picked up immediately in this handsome cowboy. She had thought him to be eighteen or so, younger than her nineteen.

"Excuse me Mr. Young," Bill said. "This is my daughter, Elizabeth."

James took his hat off. "Nice to meet you Elizabeth."

"Call me Liz. That's what my friends do."

"Yes Ma'am."

"Now then," Mr. Riley said. "Where have you worked?"

"Lazy S way down south and later, the Double D near San Antonio."

"San Antonio, huh? I've a good friend that has a small spread near there. Bill Ross and the Rocking B Ranch. We rode together with the Rangers a few years back."

Adam swallowed hard. "I've heard of it, Sir. I think its southwest of San Antonio forty or so miles."

"Dammit," he thought, *"of all the rotten luck. There is no way I can work for this man. It would be too much of a coincidence for me to show up and then that scout shows up looking for me. I'm sure Wallace told him what I look like and there ain't too many blonde cowboys. I had better ride a hell of a lot farther north."*

He looked at the girl, then at the man. He tipped his hat. "Guess I had better be riding on." He stepped off the porch and took his reins from around the wooden rail.

"I thought you were looking for work?" Bill Riley said.

"I am, but I think I want to see some country other than Texas. Maybe there's a ranch north of the Red River I can hook up with." He forked the saddle of his horse and looked at the man and then at his daughter. He tipped his hat to her. "Maybe I will see you again Liz." He reined his mount around and headed north.

"That is the strangest man I ever met," Liz mumbled.

"I've a feeling there is more to that man than just a cowboy looking for work. I don't know, but his whole attitude changed when I mentioned Ross and the Rocking B. He scratched his head and walked back in. Liz stood there, leaning against a post watching the best looking man she had ever seen, ride out of her life.

Chapter Eight

Tye whistled. He saw "Wallace looking in his direction and he motioned him to come over. A few seconds later the man was beside Tye. Tye pointed to the ground.

"This is where he left." He dismounted, kneeled and traced the tracks with his finger. He looked east. "Have you ever been in that part of the country?"

"Can't say I have." He dismounted and kneeled beside Tye and looked at the tracks. "Several hours old ain't they?"

"At least four, maybe a couple more." Tye said. Tye stood up and took his canteen from the saddle. He tipped the canvas covered jug to his mouth, swallowed a small amount, then poured some in his hat, and gave Sandy a drink. While Sandy nosily sucked up the water, Wallace gave his horse some water too.

Wallace had watched Tye for days, ever since the first time they got on the outlaw's trail with Bill and Lester. The man moved like a big cat just as he remembered Tye's pa doing when they were in the same company with the Rangers. The scout moved quietly wherever he went, and wasted no effort doing anything that wasn't necessary. He was big too, just like his pa had been. As a matter of fact, they looked almost identical. The man sure as hell knew scouting and tracking. He wondered about all the stories he had heard about him. They would talk tonight after settling in camp. He looked at the sun and figured they had three hours of daylight left.

"The tracks will be easy to follow with the ground damp, so let's make up some time before we have to make camp," Tye suggested. They followed at a steady gallop, staying just left of the tracks.

~

Miles west of Tye and Wallace, Dan signaled McClellan to halt the patrol. A large number of buzzards were circling ahead and he wanted to investigate what was attracting the deplorable scavengers. He figured it was another mess left by the Apaches and it would be hard to read what happened if the tracks of the patrol muddled things. Since leaving Fort Clark early yesterday they had come across two homesteads where settlers had been massacred. The patrol, led by Captain McClellan, had been dispatched by Major Thurston to investigate reported Apache depredations northwest of Fort Clark, it being close to the Mexican border. McClellan's orders were specific: find out if the reports were true, and if true, follow the renegades and put an end to them.

The Apaches had turned south after hitting the last
homestead, crossed the Old Mail Road, and struck another
homestead. They left nothing but mutilated bodies. Where Dan
now sat was five miles farther south of the last burned homestead.
He nudged his horse, and moved toward the circling birds.

When almost beneath the circling scavengers, he saw what
had attracted them. He felt sick. Dead horses, and the bodies of
four blue-clad troopers, and a civilian lay scattered about, scalped
and stripped of weapons. He recognized Woody Strokes, a friend
of his and a fellow scout. Woody had been sent by Major Thurston,
along with 2nd Lieutenant Harrison and three soldiers three days
ago to find Tye's trail. They were to assist him in the capture of the
outlaw after the wounded rancher, Bill Ross, had reached the fort,
and told the story of what had happened at the crossing.

From the condition of the bodies, they had been dead only
three or four hours. It looked like they had been ambushed. Stokes
and the Lieutenant lay side by side. Behind them lay three men.
Dan would bet money they never got off a shot. He muttered a
curse, and rode back to where he could see the patrol. He motioned
for them to come.

"What did you find?" McClellan asked Dan when he rode
up.

"Scout Stokes, 2nd Lieutenant Harrison, and three
troopers...dead. They were ambushed and from the position of the

horses and men, I don't think they even had a chance to get off a shot."

"DAMN!" McClellan cursed as he kicked his horse to get him moving.

"It's not a pretty sight, Captain," Dan said.

"It never is, Dan," McClellan replied. "It never is." A minute later, McClellan sat on his mount looking at the sickening sight and cursed again. "Damn the Apache…damn this land." He turned in the saddle. "Sergeant Christian, get a detail to care for these soldiers. I want them wrapped in blankets. Send a man back to Clark, and bring a wagon to take the bodies back to the fort.

"Yes, Sir," Christian said, snapping a quick salute to the captain. He turned and shouted orders to the men. The dead soldiers were quickly wrapped in blankets, and then tied securely with rope. They were placed in the shade of a huge boulder which would help keep them from becoming too 'ripe' before the wagon returned. Christian assigned one man to remain with the bodies until the wagon arrived. The fort was only four hours away, so Private Hawkins should be back with the wagon a little after midnight. Private Hawkins lived in the area around Fort Clark before he joined the army. He would not have any problem finding his way back to this spot.

"If I live to be a hundred, I'll never get used to this," McClellan said to Dan. He wiped his face with his gold colored kerchief.

"I've been out here all my life, Captain and seen this many times. A man never gets use to it. You try to accept it as that's the way it is…and will be for awhile. Men have been killing men since the days of the Bible. There have been wars over possession of land, over opposing ideas like the one we just had in our country over slavery; there have been wars over religion, and a dozen other things. I suspect it will always be that way."

McClellan sat relaxed on his horse, his hand resting on the pommel of his saddle. He looked at his scout and forced a smile. "Dan, you just said more words in a minute than I have heard you speak in the last two years." He knew Dan was an uneducated man and wondered how he knew about wars over religion. "If you don't mind me asking, how do you know about other wars, and why they were fought?"

"Tye and me spent a lot of nights around the campfire. Tye never went to school same as me, but his parents, especially his mother made sure he knew the basics of reading, writing and numbers. She also read to him a lot…stories from the Bible and from old books about a king who took soldiers clad in armor to what was a 'Holy War' in some far away country several centuries ago. I forget who the king was.

"King Arthur," McClellan said.

"That's him," Dan said excitedly. "You read about him too?"

"Sure. In school, reading about King Arthur and his knights in armor was required."

"I'll be damned," Dan replied. He turned in the saddle and looked at the men behind them waiting the order to move out. "We had better get moving Captain."

McClellan turned in the saddle, looked at the men, raising his hand as he turned back and dropping it gave the order.

"BY THE TWO'S...YO!" The patrol moved out and Dan raced ahead to take his position out in front. There was still an hour of daylight left and a few miles could be covered prior to making camp. The trail of the Apache was clear as twenty or so horses made it that way. Urgency was the order of the day, because the Apache were not resting, and Dan knew tomorrow would probably bring more tragic scenes like the ones they had observed the last two days.

~~

Adam had pushed his mount hard since leaving the rancher and his daughter. It was nearing dark and he figured he had better be looking for a place to bed down for the night. He was still cussing his bad luck. That ranch back there probably would have been a great place to work. He shut his eyes and saw Liz's face and it reminded him just how good life might have been.

He found a ten foot deep draw about twenty yards wide. Its pool of muddy water and grass, made it as good of spot as any. The sides of the draw would shield a small fire, and his horse could have all the muddy water he wanted. He filled his coffee pot with water before the horse messed it up more than it was. He took a pan and placed his kerchief over the top. He poured the water into the pan from the coffee pot, letting the kerchief strain some of the mud out. He figured boiling the water would make it okay to drink.

By the time he had unsaddled, picketed his horse, and rolled out his bedroll, the coffee was ready. He placed his small skillet on the fire, as well as some of the bacon that Mrs. Wilson had given him. He took a biscuit and soaked it in the hot grease and sat back, leaning against the rocky wall. While drinking coffee, eating the biscuit and bacon, he did some thinking about the last few days, plus what he was going to do now.

What had happened was over, and there is nothing I can do about it. I was stupid, but now I need to figure out a plan on what I am going to do. I can't believe every rancher in Texas used to be a damn Ranger like Ross and Riley. I should be able to find one that isn't. I figure I am three, maybe four days from the Red River.

If I can't find a job by then, surely I can get' lost' on the other side and find a brand to ride for. A brand to ride for...that's damn funny. Riding for the brand' or being loyal to the brand was what was expected of a cowboy. I thought I was, but...oh hell, I don't want to even think about it.

The smart thing to do would be to hide and see if that scout is following me, or not. I may be worrying about a lot of things unnecessarily if he's not. If he is, the prudent thing to do would be to shoot him, and be done with it." He thought about that for a second. *"I'm not sure I could do that even if I had the chance. I'm a cowboy, not a damn bushwhacker and murderer. I think the best thing to do is to by pass all homesteads between here and the Red River, and not leave anyone that can tell the scout they saw me. I will find work...its just going to be farther north than I anticipated."*

He finished his biscuit and bacon, emptied his coffee cup, and sat the pot on a rock close to the fire, the coals keeping it warm till in the morning. By then, the coffee should be strong enough to stand a spoon upright in , or dissolve it. He smiled and lay down on his bedroll, pulling the wool blanket up to his chin and quickly going to sleep.

~~~

Second Chance

Tye and Wallace had followed Adam until almost dark before setting up camp. After eating some jerky and a biscuit, they sat on their bedrolls drinking coffee. Even though there had been no Apache trouble this far north there was always the chance of a Comanche or Kiowa hunting party passing by, and would not pass up the chance to kill two white-eyes who were stupid enough to give their position away by building a huge fire. Tye had his usual small fire, with rocks stacked around it to shield the flames from prying eyes.

"Who's the worst man you ever brought in, Tye?" Wallace asked.

"I've tracked down several that were pretty vicious," Tye answered, "But if I had to pick it would be easy to name the top two: Alex Vasquez because of what he did to a payroll detail, or Yancey Cates who never thought twice about killing a man, woman, or child. If I penned it down to one, it probably would have to be Yancey because of the number of people he killed for no reason. He even killed men in his own gang."

"I know Ben was killed after I left the Rangers. I knew how good he was at scouting and fighting, and always figured he would never be killed. How did it happen, if you don't mind talking about it?"

Tye thought about it for a minute. "I haven't talked about it for a long time, Wallace." Tye took a couple sips of coffee and stood up, emptying his cup in the fire. Sparks spewed into the air and smoke billowed up. Wallace wondered if he had made a mistake in asking that question. Finally Tye spoke. "We had been in a continuous running fight with some Comanche for most of the day. It was late, and a camp had been set up. Pa and I had just returned to get a little rest, when word arrived that five men were pinned down about two miles from where we were. Pa jumped up, and said he would see what the situation was and took some men with him, including me. I was nineteen, and very young compared to most of the men who, for the most part, were about pa's age or older." He laughed a little and said, "Everyone was always trying to protect me like I was their son."

It was Wallace's turn to laugh. "I had already left the Rangers by then, but I remember you as a youngster, and I know what you are talking about when you say everyone tried to keep you out of trouble."

Tye chuckled. "Anyway, we found the trapped men, and they were in a hell of a fix. The Comanche knew they had them in their clutches. If all of the Comanche had rifles instead of bows, they would have already been dead. The men were trapped in a draw, which normally might have offered good protection, but this particular one had high ground around it, so the Comanche were keeping the men pinned down by firing a continuous rain of arrows, and an occasional bullet on them from this high ground.

Second Chance

We were behind the warriors on the north side of the draw, but we were in danger of being seen by the ones on the south side if we advanced any closer. It appeared to be a hopeless situation, but you know pa, he always had an answer for every problem and if he didn't, he made you think he did."

"The men in the draw appeared to be afoot as several dead horses could be seen. We had fifteen men and it looked like the Comanches had fifty or so. We split our group with five men going in to get the trapped men while the other ten put down a covering fire. The men going in left their rifles with the ten giving each man two rounds of rifle fire, plus their pistols. The five going in were to use their pistols, as the fighting would be close in. Pa was one of the five, and wouldn't let me go. The five going in would pick up the trapped men with each riding double."

"When we were in position, we opened up on the warriors on the north side, their backs to us. The Rangers, as you know, were a mixed group of men: some were trappers, some were buffalo hunters, some were lawmen, and some were outlaws, but they all had one thing in common…they could shoot the eyes out of a turkey at fifty paces. I'm not sure how many Comanche went down with the first two volleys but there weren't many misses. Pa and the other four rode through them, riding hard, each man lying low in the saddle offering as small a target as possible. The surviving braves on our side scattered, but the ones on the other side were more than upset when they saw what was happening and kept raining raining a lot of lead and arrows down on the five men. But somehow, every man made it into the draw and out, each with a comrade hanging on behind them."

"We fired our pistols trying to keep the warriors behind the rocks, but like all warriors, they paid no attention to the danger of being killed, and continued firing. None of us could believe the men would get out alive, but they did. Hollering and laughing, they were a happy lot until they saw pa. They knew they were alive because of his crazy plan. He had taken a bullet in the chest, but somehow stayed on his horse, and got his men to safety. Every man came by while pa lay dying in my arms, and they all shook his hand."

Wallace shook his head. "He was a man, Tye. A man that anyone would have been proud to call a friend. A man that one could depend on when things got rough. That's the way I seen him."

"Thanks Wallace. I appreciate those words."

"From what I hear, you have that same respect from the men and women in the area around Fort Clark, as well as the soldiers stationed there."

"One thing I learned from pa was to try and help my neighbors because one never knows when you may need help yourself."

Second Chance

Tye sat back down on his bedroll. "Let's get some sleep. Maybe we can catch up with Adam tomorrow."

"Does one of us need to stay awake?" Wallace asked.

"Sandy and your horse are ten feet away. I promise you they will let us know if someone or something gets close to camp." Both men curled up under their blanket and drifted off.

~~~

Back at Fort Clark, the morning sun brought a huge smile to the face of young Todd Jenkins as he climbed out of bed. Major Thurston had given Todd a present yesterday; the sorrel that Todd had rescued from the wrangler who was mistreating him. Not only had the major given him the horse, but also a saddle. This morning, he was going for a ride on the first horse he could call his own.

After eating a quick breakfast, he ran to the stables to saddle Lucky, the name he had given the sorrel. Todd figured it was an appropriate name since the horse was lucky he was there to prevent him from being beaten. Lucky came to him just as soon as Todd stepped on the lower rung of the corral fence. The horse nuzzled his shoulder and nickered. Todd jumped over the fence and made his way to the tack room where he found his saddle, blanket, and bridle. He saddled Lucky and walked him through the gate, closing it behind him. He then mounted and made his way to the bridge over Los Moras Creek, and out onto the Old Mail Road.

He kicked Lucky on the flanks and they were off, heading west out of Brackettville at a fast gallop.

Riding easy, feeling the wind in his face, Todd was as happy as he had ever been. Todd gave Lucky his head and the horse responded, running full out. *"Man...he can run,"* Todd thought as the sage, cactus, and mesquite became just a blur in his peripheral vision as he kept his eyes ahead. He let him run for less than a minute, and then reined him to a trot, and then a walk. He leaned forward, whispering in Lucky's ear as he stroked his new friend's neck. Lucky nickered and nodded his head, bringing a smile to Todd's face.

He was three or so miles from the Fort when he decided to turn back. He had promised Sergeant O'Malley he would not ride any farther. He really liked the old sergeant and had tremendous respect for him. He appreciated what he and Mrs. O'Malley had done for him, and was doing for him. Looking down the road he saw a single rider coming toward him. He thought nothing of it as the road was well traveled.

At thirty yards, he suspected the man was probably an ex-buffalo hunter. He was huge, and his heavy fur coat made from buffalo hide made him look even larger. His face was covered by a black beard, and on his head was a filthy gray hat, the brim turned up, pinned to the crown. He had gray wool pants, and the same Apache type moccasin boots that Tye wore.

"That's a fine looking horse you got there young feller," the man said when they reached a few feet apart.

"Thanks," Todd answered. "His name is Lucky…and you're right, he is a fine animal."

"Lucky!" The big man thought, and then smiled. *"That's an appropriate name for my new mount."* When he was beside Todd, he removed his left foot from the stirrup, and with no warning, kicked Todd, catching the boy by surprise and knocking him out of the saddle. The youngster hit the ground hard on his back, knocking the wind out of him. The big man slid out of the saddle, and as Todd raised himself up on his hands and knees the man kicked him in the side, the side where he had been shot three months earlier. Pain wracked his body and he could not seem to get his breath. Tears welled up and he could not see clearly. He felt a hand grab the collar of his coat and was jerked to his feet. He vaguely saw the man's face through his tears and swung hard with his right fist, like Tye had taught him. It was a short, hard punch, not one of those roundhouse types most men used, and he had his weight behind it. His fist struck the bearded man on the left cheek. It was a solid blow and felt good to strike back, but only for a second. The man screamed out a curse and hit Todd several times in the face, shoulders, and stomach. Todd felt himself falling, as everything went black.

The man grabbed the unconscious Todd by the collar again, and dragged him off the road, laying him behind cactus and thick sage. He cursed again, as he rubbed his cheek where the boy had struck him. It had been a hard lick. He remounted his horse, grabbed Lucky's reins and continued west down the Old Mail Road.

~~

The sun had barely peeked over the horizon when Tye and Wallace approached the best looking ranch house either had ever seen. Tye called out.

"Hello the house!" Immediately they saw two rifles appear at the open windows on each side of the door. "Just want to talk," say said loud enough for them to hear and raised his hands and nudges Sandy into moving toward the house. Wallace followed Tye's lead. The door opened and a man at least six-foot-five stepped out holding a Colt in his right hand.

"Who are you and what do you want?"

"Tye Watkins and this here is Wallace Anderson," Tye answered.

"You the Watkins from Fort Clark?"

"Yes Sir!" The man holstered his Colt and told the people with the rifles to relax. "Heard of you. Step down and come on in the house." Both men stepped from the saddle and approached the porch where the man stood. He big rancher stuck out his hand when Tye stepped on the porch. "Bill Riley," he said shaking Tye's and Wallace's hand. "Do I know you," he asked as he shook Wallace's hand?

"I was with the Rangers when you and Bill Ross rode with them. I work for Ross on the Rocking B down by San Antonio."

"Of course. I remember. How are the old cuss and his family doing?

"Not well, Bill. His place was robbed, his wife and son murdered while he was away buying supplies. He is lying in the hospital in Fort Clark. He was wounded in a shoot-out with the thieves. All were killed, thanks to Tye, except one. We've followed his track to here.

"Here!" Riley exclaimed.

"We've been on his trail," Tye said, "And his tracks led right to your door step."

"What did this fellow look like?"

Wallace answered. "Young, good looking with blonde hair."

"I knew it. I knew something was wrong with that kid."

"You saw him?" Tye asked.

"Yeah I saw him. Hell, the bastard sat right there on my porch late yesterday. I offered him a job. I knew something was wrong, because when he was telling me he worked on several ranches around San Antonio, I mention I knew Bill Ross, who owned the Rocking B, and his whole attitude changed. Said he thought he would look farther north, maybe across the Red River, for work."

"The son-of-a-bitch worked for Mr. Ross. They treated him like family, and he turned on them," Anderson said, outrage apparent in his tone of voice. "My good friend, Lester, and me was on their trail with Mr. Ross. Lester was also wounded in the shoot out."

"Are they going to be alright," Riley asked

Tye answered. "Yeah, Lester's wound was just a flesh wound on his shoulder, but Ross was hit hard, high in the right upper chest. Luckily, the bullet went clean through and missed his lungs. It was painful, but with care and rest, he'll be alright."

Riley seem to relax somewhat. "I can't believe I almost hired the man." A pretty young girl appeared with some coffee. "This here is my daughter, Elizabeth."

Both men took off their hats. "My friends call me Liz," she said, handing the three men cups which she then filled with coffee.

"Thank you ma'am," Tye and Wallace both said at the same time.

"We're going to have breakfast pretty soon if ya'll can stay," Riley said.

Tye shook his head. "We'll finish our coffee and get back on the trail. Thanks for the offer."

"My son told me where he saw where the man left our ranch. The least I can do is take you there where you don't have to spend time looking for his tracks leaving."

"We'd appreciate that," Tye said as he and Wallace handed their cups to Liz. The two men sat on their horses waiting for Bill to saddle his. They rode north, away from the ranch house.

"Nice spread you have here Mr. Riley," Anderson said looking back at the house.

"Thanks Wallace. If you ever leave Ross, come up here."

"That's not going to happen. Me and old Lester have known that old cuss too long. We're more than just friends, sorter like family."

Riley nodded. "You tell Bill I said hello and to make sure he stops by if he's ever up this way," Riley said as he reined his mount in. "There's his tracks like my son said."

Tye and Wallace shook the rancher's hand. "Thanks for the hospitality," Tye said, "And for putting us on the trail."

"You're more than welcome and I hope you find the son-of-a-bitch. As far as I'm concerned, it's the lowest form of man who turns on the brand he is riding for. Good luck!" He watched as Tye and Wallace rode off at a gallop, following the tracks that were plain as day on the damp ground

~~

Adam lay under the wool blanket for two hours after the sun arose. He was warm and comfortable, and saw no need to hurry. Lying there, he heard a rumbling sound, like distant thunder. He sat up and looked at the sky in all directions, but there were no clouds. The sound grew louder and he became concerned about a stampede of cattle, or perhaps some of the scattered buffalo herds that were still around. He pulled on his boots, and made his way to where he could see over the rim of the ravine he was camped in. Peering over the rim he immediately dropped down, feeling sick to his stomach. Fear does that to a man sometimes. What he saw was maybe a hundred warriors two hundred yards away riding south. He quickly looked at his campfire and saw it was out completely.

"Thank God I did not make coffee." Panic rose in him suddenly. *"OH MY GOD, the way they are traveling they will cross my tracks and follow them here."* He quickly saddled his horse, checked his weapons, and jumped onto the saddle. He raced his horse out of the ravine and headed north.

~~

Tye and Wallace left before it was full light. The tracks were plain, even in the faint light of pre-dawn. They had been traveling fast, alternating between a gallop, canter, and walking. The horses were holding up well, and Tye hoped they were closing the gap. He would never guess that a man on the run would lie in camp two hours after the sun came up, and that they had cut the time in more than half. They would not realize that until they found his camp, and saw how fresh the tracks were.

Both men reined in at the same time. They stared at he ground ahead of them, unbelieving at what they saw. A tremendous area was trampled under a large number of horses-unshod horses. They quickly dismounted after looking in all directions for trouble. The tracks were no more than an hour old. Circling the area, Tye figured the Indians had come across Adams tracks and stopped, milling about while deciding what to do. From reading the sign he saw it looked like the main party continued south with five warriors sent to follow the white man's tracks.

They followed the tracks to the ravine where Adam had camped. Again, reading sign and guessing the rest, Tye had a good idea what happened.

"Our friend spent an hour or so longer in camp than he should have. He saw the Indians when they rode by over there." He pointed with his Henry where the Indians had passed by Adam's camp. "He was smart enough to figure they would see his tracks and lit out of here at a dead run. The Indians, I'm guessing Comanche, found the tracks and five of them are after him now." He mounted Sandy and added. "We are only an hour or so behind them." They kicked their mounts into a gallop. Tye looked at Wallace. "Keep your eyes open for trouble. We don't want to stumble into five Comanche by accident." Wallace nodded.

~~

Dan sat on his horse looking around the abandoned camp. He was where the Apaches had camped last night. They had left two hours earlier, three at the most. He heard the patrol coming, and smiled as a thought crossed his mind. *"It's like Tye said before. The army will never surprise the Apache, because the Apache can hear them a mile away. Besides, it seemed the Apache somehow communicated with the hawks, and other birds who would tell them where their enemy was."* He knew this was stupid to think like that, but then again, the Apache always seemed to be a step ahead of the army.

"We're gaining ground, Captain," he said, when McClellan and the patrol arrived.

"How close?" McClellan asked.

"Two…maybe three hours. Close enough to be careful. If they left a man behind watching for trouble, and if he spotted us, they could have a surprise for us." The captain turned in his saddle.

"Sergeant Christian! Corporal Payne!" he hollered. Both men came in a hurry. "Have the men stay alert. Dan here says we are no more than two or so hours behind the Apache. Both of you know what that could mean, so have the men ready." Both men gave a quick salute, reined their mounts around, and returned to the men shouting orders. The Sharps came out of the saddle scabbards, and each man checked to be sure his was in working order. The Colt revolvers each man carried were checked too.

~~

Senior Master Sergeant O'Malley paced back and forth in front of the stables back at Fort Clark. He was worried. Todd said he would be gone only an hour or so, and that was two hours ago. It wasn't like the youngster not to do what he said he would do. He paced a few more minutes, and then turned to one of the soldiers on stable duty. "Get my horse and get him saddled. I'll be back in a minute." Without waiting for an answer, he turned and headed for Post Headquarters, and Major Thurston.

Five minutes later he was in Thurston's office. The major was surprised, but glad to see O'Malley. O'Malley was his right hand man. He was one hell of a soldier, as well as the best drill sergeant Thurston had ever seen.

"Good to see you, Sergeant." Thurston immediately saw from O'Malley's expression that something was bothering the old soldier.

"Sir," O'Malley said. "Todd left this morning on the horse you gave him yesterday. He was so excited I bet he didn't sleep last night, for he hurried through his breakfast, and headed for the stables just about the time the sun broke over the horizon. He told me he would not be gone for more than an hour or so. The boy always does what he says he's going to do. He's not back, Sir, and it's been two and a half hours and I'm worried something happened."

"Are you asking me for permission to leave the fort and look for him?"

O'Malley nodded. "Yes Sir."

Thurston put his hand on his sergeant's shoulder. "Go ahead. If there is anything wrong, let me know immediately."

O'Malley nodded, saluted, and hurried out the door. Thurston smiled and shook his head. He worries about that boy, and the Turley kids, just like they were his own blood. He sat down at his desk and mumbled. "That speaks well of a man who can take in kids that have no place to go, and raise them as his own. "*Yep!*" He mused. "*It takes quite a man to do that and by*

God, O'Malley is a man. I hope that boy is just having a lot of fun, and time got away from him.

O'Malley found his horse saddled, and ready, when he arrived at the stables. Mounting him, he crossed the bridge over Los Moras Creek and headed west on The Old Mail Road. He had told Todd to stay on the road and under no circumstances, was he to leave it. *"I pray he listened to me and did as I asked,"* he thought.

He had been out here a long time, but had always left the tracking and sign reading to Tye and his scouts. He had listened to them enough though, that he knew the basics of how to tell a story of what happened by tracks and other signs. Hell, Tye could go into a camp and tell you how many men had been there, what they ate, how many horses they had, the direction they had left in, and how long they had been gone. Even though he was worried sick about Todd, he chuckled as a thought crossed his mind.

"If I ever asked him, he could probably tell me what they had talked about too."

He rode in the middle of the road, but was not paying much attention to the tracks on the road. He was looking on both sides of the road for tracks leaving it. He had gone about two miles when he pulled up. Something caught his eye that wasn't right. He sat and looked all around him. Something had happened here. He dismounted and holding his mount's reins in his left hand, kneeled and studied the ground. He wished Tye was here, because he could figure it out in a minute. It looked like someone had fallen off his horse, because he could see hand prints in the dirt on the road. The ground was torn up some, and there were two sets of tracks; large tracks that were deep, like the man was heavy and also smaller tracks. A chill went up O'Malley's spine.

"Todd...those small tracks are Todd's." He stood up, and looking at the ground saw what looked like tracks of something or someone being dragged off the road. O'Malley followed the tracks with his eyes to the brush on the side of the road and saw what looked like a boot partially showing from behind a thick sage bush. He froze, unable to move for a few seconds. Taking a deep breath, he slowly walked to the bush, his body shaking, afraid of what he was going to find on the other side. "God, please...please God, don't let him be dead," he prayed.

Chapter Nine

Adam, wanting to put as much distance as possible between him and the Indians, pushed his horse way to hard. The horse was almost to the point of floundering before Adam realized his mistake. Knowing it would kill the horse to continue, he reined him in. He sat for a moment, taking time to study the terrain around him.

A quarter of a mile away, he saw a hill that stood above those around it. Its steep slopes and large boulders would prevent the Indians from a mounted charge to the top. He twisted in the saddle looking at his back trail. He saw no sign of the Indians, but he had a feeling in his gut they were coming. Dismounting, he took a quick inspection of his horse's condition. Satisfied the horse would be fine with a little rest, he led him to the base of the hill. After removing the saddle and bedroll, he hid them in some brush on the edge of a draw. He brushed his tracks away the best he could with a mesquite limb as he walked back to his horse. After hobbling the horse and giving him some water, Adam, after gathering up his canteen, saddle bags, and rifle, began his climb up the hill.

Once on top, he looked south for signs of trouble coming. Seeing no Indians, he thought it best to take a look-see around the top of the hill and find where his best defensive position would be. There were large boulders scattered about that offered protection. He also realized they would do the same for any Indian that managed to get to the top. He picked a spot in the shade of a large boulder that offered a clear view south, where he figured trouble would be coming.

~~

Tye and Wallace held their mounts to an easy gallop, as they followed the tracks of the five Indian ponies. They reined their horses to a walk as they approached the top of a hill. Stopping to let their horse's blow a little, Tye dismounted, and kneeled to take a closer look at the tracks. He quickly realized they were only minutes behind the Indians.

"We're damn close Wallace. I'm going to take a look-see over the top of the next hill." Wallace nodded and Tye trotted toward the crest of the hill. When he was near the top, he dropped to a crouch, then to his belly, and crawled forward. He sure as hell did not want to be sky-lined by standing on the top of the hill like an idiot where a half-blind Indian could see him.

Second Chance

Five Indians were a quarter of a mile away, riding with
their backs to him. While he watched, they stopped; one
dismounted, and kneeled to the ground.

"*Something got their attention,* Tye thought. The one on
the ground remounted, and headed north with the others following.
Tye hurried back to Wallace.

~~

Adam held his breath as he watched the Indians around his
horse. As he watched, all five Indians looked at the top of the hill.
The Comanche, or what ever tribe they were, sat on their ponies at
the base staring right where Adam was hidden. He was in the
shadows, and suspected the Indians could not see him. They might
though, if he moved, so he sat there, not moving, not breathing, not
even blinking-scared to death. One Indian slid off his pony, and
walked to the base of the hill. After kneeling down looking for
tracks, he quickly straightened up and pointed to the top. Adam
knew he was in trouble now. With the Indians in plain view, he
decided to try and lower the odds some. He quickly raised his
rifle, and fired at the nearest warrior. His hurried shot missed and
in an instant, the Indians disappeared among the boulders.

~~

West of Fort Clark, Sergeant O'Malley took a deep breath, and pushed the sage bush's branches aside. Looking over the top, his worst fears were realized. Todd lay there, blood on his face, not moving. O'Malley, fearing the worse, let the branches fall back and stepping around the bush, kneeled beside the boy. Tears filled his eyes as he looked to heaven.

"Why God...why?"

As he stared at the sky, he heard a moan. Slowly he lowered his gaze to Todd and saw the lad's chest rising and falling.

"He's alive! MY GOD, HE'S ALIVE," he yelled. He scooped the unconscious boy into his arms, and carried him to his horse. Lifting Todd onto his right shoulder, he stepped into the stirrup and into the saddle. He slid the boy off his shoulder onto his thighs and then held him against his chest like one would a baby. He reined his horse around, heading east on the road toward Fort Clark.

~~

Tye and Wallace heard the crack of a rifle. The sound came from just over the next hill. Both men dismounted and headed up the slope to take a look. They saw the Indians in the rocks at the base of a huge hill.

"What's going on?" Wallace asked.

"They have a man, probably Adam, trapped on the hill." As he spoke, they watched the Indians spread out around the base of the hill. The warriors immediately began making their way up the steep slope. The two men could only see the warriors now and then as they moved from boulder to boulder, staying out of sight from above as only an Indian could.

Tye's mind was working fast, trying to figure out how he and Wallace could get close without drawing the Indians fire. The problem was solved as shots rang out from the top of the hill, and return fire came from the Indians.

"Let's get the hell over there quick while they have all their attention on the man on the hill," Tye said as he headed back down the slope to the horses. Reaching the bottom, they leaped into their saddles, put their horses in a dead run up the slope and down the other side toward the hill a quarter of a mile away.

~~

Miles away from where Tye and Wallace were, Dan reined his mount in hard, as shots suddenly came from in front, and not far away. He twisted in the saddle and signaled the patrol to hold up. As he rode forward, the rifle fire became louder and he could hear the distinctive screams of the Apache.

"They have hit another homestead," he thought. *"At least these people were not surprised and are putting up a fight."* The battle sounded as if it was just over the rise so he rode back, signaling McClellan and the patrol to come to him.

He quickly explained what was happening to the captain. McClellan turned and shouted,

"Form a skirmish line on me, pistols only. The men quickly spread out in a line on both sides of the captain. Dan was beside McClellan, and Sergeant Christian and Corporal Payne were on the opposite ends of the line. They would keep the men from spreading out to much, leaving gaps in the ranks. McClellan turned to his bugler. "Sound the order to charge when we top that rise in front of us and not before." The corporal nodded. McClellan stood in the stirrups and shouted, "FOLLOW ME." He led the men up the rise at a canter. Reaching the tope of the hill, the men saw the homestead no more than seventy-five to a hundred yards away. A large number of screaming Apaches were riding back and forth shooting arrows and firing rifles at the people barricaded in the house.

The bugler sounded charge and immediately the patrol was in an all out run down the slope. Troopers began firing their pistols from forty or so yards away. The Apaches, who had been so intent on killing the people in the homestead, did not see the soldiers until the bugle sounded, and by the time they could react, the soldiers were almost upon them.

A few of the bullets from the soldier's pistols found their marks, but most missed. Hitting anything from a running horse was mostly luck anyway . The Apache however, were not running, and they fired an accurate volley of bullets and arrows in the direction of the charging bluecoats. Five soldiers were knocked from their mounts, and two more slumped in their saddles.

As the two groups came together, it was a soldier's worse nightmare-hand to hand combat with Apaches. The Indians were leaping from their pony's backs, hitting the troopers like battering rams, knocking men from their saddles, then slashing at the soldiers as they lay on the ground with knives or tomahawks. Smoke from the guns, and dust from the horses hooves, blanketed the area. Screams from wounded men joined the shouts of angry Apaches. Dan fired his pistol into the face of an Apache warrior that was trying to drag him from the saddle. McClelland emptied his pistol, shifted the empty gun to his left hand, and swung his saber with his right, slashing his way through the warriors who were trying to knock him from his horse.

Corporal Payne was trying to make sure none of the warriors escaped around his end of the line, and had downed two with his pistol. His head was suddenly jerked backwards by a hand on his forehead. A warrior had jumped on his horse behind him.

Instinctively, he threw up his left hand to protect his throat, and the knife that was intended for his jugular cut deep into his forearm. He twisted his body, extended his gun hand across his body, pointed the gun backwards, and pulled the trigger. The flash from the pistol burned his shirt and skin under his left ribs, but the grunt of the Apache told him his bullet found a home. The hand that had held his head fell away, as the body of the warrior tumbled from the back of his horse.

Christian was doing his best to hold back any warriors trying to escape his way. His horse was shot, stumbled and fell, pinning the sergeant's right leg underneath. He had no choice but to fight where he was. The Apache were everywhere; one Apache lay dead across his horse's neck and another lay on the ground at the rear of the horse. Two more came from the dust and smoke at him, no more than fifteen feet away. He knocked one down with a quick shot from his revolver, but the other was on him before he could swing the barrel and line him up. He rolled his upper body to the side just as the war club hit the ground where his head had been an instant earlier. The Apache, now straddling Christian, raised the club again, intending to bash in the bluecoat's head. Christian, using the heavy Navy Colt like a club, struck the warrior hard in the left knee cap. The brave screamed in pain and dropped his club as he grabbed his knee. Christian shot him in the chest. The Apache warrior fell on top of him, his sweaty, bloody chest across

Christian's face. The sergeant got his arms under the Apache and lifted him off. The sergeant lay looked quickly around, expecting another warrior to come at him, but then he realized how quiet it had become. The only sound was the nickering of wounded horses, and the moans of wounded men. The slight breeze was slowly blowing the dust and smoke away. For the men still standing, the scene unfolding was horrific. From where Christian lay, he could see no Apaches standing, and only seven blue clad men along with Dan. He saw McClellan standing in the center of the bloody scene. He was holding his left arm with his right, which still held his saber, blood dripping from its tip. A knife could be seen stuck in his upper left arm.

McClellan, looking around, could not believe the carnage. A few feet in front of where he stood, lay private Jessup, a knife in his chest with a dead Apache's grip still around the handle. Slowly turning around, he stumbled across another trooper with the side of his head caved in. He looked at the house, just as a man and two boys came out followed by a woman. The older man walked directly to him and took him by the shoulder trying to lead him to his house. McClellan pulled away. "My men... help me with my men." He staggered a couple of steps and sat down, his chin resting on his chest.

The man shouted to his sons.

"Get the wounded in the house so your ma can tend to them. He bent down and lifted the captain to his feet. "We'll take care of your men Captain. You come with me." He helped McClellan inside the house.

Two soldiers and Payne were with Christian, trying to get the sergeant's leg out from under the dead horse. All three men saw the dead Apaches lying around the sergeant, and knew the man was lucky to be alive. A couple minutes later, the horse was lifted enough to get Christian's leg out. As soon as the weight of the horse was lifted off, the pain hit. His leg was broken just above the ankle. The men helped him into the house. Everywhere Corporal Payne looked, there was a wounded soldier. Eleven men lay on the floor bleeding from various wounds, some serious and others minor, but painful. The lady was an angel, rushing from man to man, cleaning wounds, bandaging wounds, and offering words of encouragement.

As she bandaged the cut on his arm, Payne cringed as he watched the knife pulled from Captain McClellan's arm by the woman's husband. He also noticed the officer was last to be doctored. He saw the other man watching as the knife was removed. Payne remembered that a few short months ago, McClellan was an arrogant officer that thought he was better than anyone else. The enlisted men could not stand him. On one patrol, he ignored Tye's warnings and stupidly led his men into an ambush. All would have been killed if Tye had not managed to pull them out. It was a sobering experience for the headstrong young officer, and it changed his attitude completely. His actions on patrols since that humbling moment had resulted in his becoming a favorite among the enlisted men, and Major Thurston's most dependable and trusted officer.

Seven soldiers were dead along with twenty-two Apaches. The dead soldiers were wrapped in blankets and the Apaches were stacked in a corner of the yard. Twenty-five soldiers and Dan had attacked the Apaches, and now seven were dead with eleven wounded. Three of the wounded would probably not make it back to Fort Clark. McClellan had a courier on his way back to Clark to fill Thurston in on the events. The Gibson family could not do enough for McClellan and the soldiers. The family knew they had been plucked from sure death by the timely arrival and sacrifice of the soldiers. The Gibson boys had gathered the guns of the dead soldiers and Indians. Among the guns taken from the Apaches were several thirteen shot Henry repeating rifles. McClellan knew the army would not let his men use them so he gave three of the guns to the Gibson's. The rifles could mean the difference in life or death for the family if another attack came. He had the other rifles wrapped in a blanket, and tied to the back of one of the dead troopers mounts. He would let the major decide what to do with them. If he lived to be a hundred he would never understand the army's refusal to do away with the old single shot Sharps, and use modern weapons such as the Henry.

~~

Tye and Wallace were less than a fifty yards from the base of the hill when one of the Indians spotted them and shouted a warning. With the first shot fired at them, Tye reined Sandy to the left and Wallace veered to the right. Two more shots came their way before they reached the rocks at the base of the hill. Quickly dismounting, both found cover. Tye, looking the situation over knew this was not going to be easy. Trying to flush out Indians from cover was always going to be hell.

"I'm going to work my way up, Wallace. Stay behind me and watch my back." Wallace nodded, and checked his Colt to make sure it was fully loaded. There was no need to carry the Henry because any shooting would be at close range. Wallace let Tye move about twenty feet above him before following. Both men were sweating despite the coolness of the morning. Tye had stopped climbing, crouched behind a huge boulder trying to decide which side to go around.

A bad decision, a wrong step, even breathing too loud in this situation could mean instant death. A normal white man would stand no chance in this game against Indians, but this scout was a long ways from normal. He was as much an Indian as the men he was hunting. He could play their game of patience and stealth as well as they could. The advantage, if there was one in a game like this, was with the Indians. They could remain hidden and wait for the white man to make a mistake.

From the top of the hill, Adam had watched the two men riding in. He recognized Wallace immediately and he suspected the big man to be Watkins. He did not fire at them because the bottom line was-he was more than happy to see them. He knew that the Indians would eventually sneak up close and rush him from all directions and he would be killed, or worse, captured. If the two men could help him escape the Indians, he would deal with them later.

~~

Sergeant O'Malley, Mrs. O'Malley, Major Thurston, Rebecca, and Buff stood around Todd's bed in the fort's hospital as the post surgeon examined the boy's wounds. Todd had not regained consciousness since O'Malley had found him. Ten minutes passed before the surgeon spoke.

"The injuries are mostly superficial with the exception of the one above his left ear. That was an exceptionally hard blow and I suspect the reason he is unconscious right now."

"Does that mean he is going to live-be alright," O'Malley asked?

The doctor shrugged his shoulders.

"I can't say Sergeant. I don't think he is in danger of dying, but with head injuries like this…" he hesitated for a few seconds. "With injuries like the one on the temple one never knows. He may wake up in the next breath or he may be unconscious for hours-maybe days. When he does wake up he may be fine or he may not know anyone or where he is for awhile. He may not remember what happened to him. Medicine can fix broken bones, heal gun shot and arrow wounds, most sicknesses, but when it comes to head injuries, medicine has not advanced that far. We will just have to wait and see. I would suggest that someone be here all the time in case he does wake up. One of my assistants or I will check in hourly around the clock until he does. Now, if you will excuse me, I have some other patients to tend to."

"Thanks Captain," Thurston said. The doctor nodded and left. No one said anything for a minute. Rebecca stood beside the bed holding one of Todd's hands, her eyes brimming with tears, flowing down her cheeks. Buff put his arm around her, and she laid her head against his shoulder.

The old trapper patted her on the back. "I know things don't look good right now, Rebecca, but Todd is going to wake up and he's going to be fine." He nodded to O'Malley. "Can you and

Mrs. O'Malley take Rebecca home? I'll stay here with Todd for awhile until one of you comes back. She needs to get some rest."

"Of course, Buff," O'Malley answered. "We'll do that. Someone will be here to relive you in a couple hours." He took Rebecca by the hand and gently pulled her away from Buff.

Buff turned his attention back to Todd. Walking over to the wash basin, he soaked a towel. Sitting back down in the chair beside the bed, he placed the cool, wet towel across the boy's forehead, leaned back and watched-thinking. His first thought was about Tye and how he would handle this situation.

"I've watched Tye become close to that boy the last three months. I suspect he is going to be upset that he was not here. I hope he has found that man he's after and is on his way back. He sure needs to be here when Todd wakes up." He looked at Todd's almost unrecognizable face: the cuts, the bruises, the swelling, and wondered what kind of man could do this to a kid.

"If Todd can remember and tell us what happened and who did this, I sure as hell would not want to be in that mans boots when Tye catches up with him." He shut his eyes and imagined what Tye would do. The picture brought a smile to his craggy face.

Chapter Ten

Tye, taking his time and being careful where he stepped, eased around the boulder. Only a man wearing moccasins could move quietly because of the loose, rocky soil. He hesitated after every step, watching for any movement, his ears tuned for any sound. After fifteen minutes he had moved up the slope only twenty feet. This was like the kids game of hide and seek only the one found would not be tagged it-he would be dead.

Wallace, watching Tye's every move, knew why the man was alive after all these years of fighting outlaws and the Apache. He moved like an Indian, blended in to the terrain like one. The man was all he had heard he was. He was watching a man that was a master in stealth. Wallace looked quickly at his own hands and they were clammy, shaking from the tension. He had fought Injuns before, but usually on open ground, not like this. He wiped his gun hand on his pants, and then quickly raised his eyes up to Tye. He watched the area to both sides of where the scout was climbing. He swore to himself. "Damn, I hate this."

Tye took a step and froze. Had he heard something, or was it his imagination? He thought he heard what sounded like the faint tick of metal on rock. He waited, not blinking, every nerve in his body tense. A minute passed-two minutes, and he slowly turned his head to the left. The heel of a moccasin was visible protruding from between two boulders about ten feet above and to the left of him. He looked down the slope at Wallace, pointed to the spot when the Indian was hidden. Wallace nodded.

Using hand signals, Tye indicated he was going to move to the right, and up to get above the warrior. Wallace nodded his understanding of Tye's intentions. He placed his right arm across the boulder he stood behind, then pointed his Colt where Tye indicated the Indian was hidden.

Adam could see the two white men below him, and he knew where the Indian was, but could not see enough of the Indian to risk a shot. Taking a quick look at Wallace, he thought he saw movement to the man's right. He wiped the sweat from his eyes and pointed the Henry where he had seen the movement-or thought he had. He watched for a minute and saw nothing but rocks. Figuring he had imagined the movement, he started to turn his attention back to the scout when he saw it again. This time, he saw the tip of a feather sticking above a boulder about ten feet from Wallace. As Adam watched, the feather moved slightly. Adam looked at Wallace. He saw the man's eyes and attention was focused on Tye. He had no idea the warrior was almost on him.

Adam sighted his rifle at the edge of the boulder the creeping Indian was hiding behind and waited. Thirty seconds later he saw part of the painted face of the warrior as he moved silently in position to strike Wallace from behind. Adam took a deep breath and placed the 'v' of the Henry's sights on where he thought the Indian would come from behind the huge rock when he attacked. He waited.

Tye moved as silently as a cat. He made sure his gun or leather buckskin shirt did not rub against the rocks. Fifteen minutes later he was above and behind the brave. He holstered his Colt, and pulled his Bowie knife from its sheath. He intended to take the Indian as quietly as possible. Just as he was making his move, he was startled by a shot from above him.

Adam pulled the trigger as soon as the Indian moved and his aim was good. His bullet caught the Indian square in the chest just as he was leaping for the unsuspecting Wallace. Wallace whirled around, saw the Indian crumple to the rocks and tumble down the rocky slope. Looking up the hill, he saw Adam waving at him. He resisted the instinct of waving back, but realized the outlaw had just saved his life.

Tye, his attention distracted for only a second, was facing the Indian who had looked up when Adam fired and saw Tye. The brave quickly turned to face his attacker. The boulder the two men were fighting behind was large. The size of it prevented Wallace from seeing what was going on, but the sound of displaced rocks and a hell of a lot of grunts could be heard.

Second Chance

Facing the Indian, Tye saw his suspicions had been correct-
Comanche. The warrior raised his rifle, but a quick kick from Tye
sent the weapon flying from his hands. Both had their knives out
and were now chest to chest, each trying to wrest his knife hand
away from the other. The brave's grip was like a vice and Tye
wasn't sure he was going to be able to jerk his hand free. The
Comanche tried the old groin mash with his knee, but Tye, seeing
that many times before, was ready. He twisted his body, catching
the knee on his hip instead of his groin. Tye fell backwards,
resulting in a slight separation between the bodies. As he fell, he
brought up his right foot and placed it in the brave's stomach. He
straightened his leg as his back hit the rocky ground and the
Comanche's grip was torn loose as he was propelled through the
air hitting the ground hard, stunning him. Tye was on him instantly
intending to finish him off, but was surprised when the warrior
caught his downward plunge of his knife with his hand, stopping
the thrust. The warrior had lost his knife when he hit the ground
and now held Tye's knife hand with both hands.

Tye, knowing he was at an impasse, struck the brave in the
face with his left fist. He struck him a second, and then a third
time before the Comanche released his grip. Instead of driving his
knife into the chest of his adversary, he reversed the knife, and
struck the man on the temple with the butt of his Bowie. Standing

up, the scout leaned against the boulder, trying to catch his breath. Wallace came to him and looked down at the Comanche.

"He dead?"

Tye shook his head, gasping for air, stammered, "Out…he's out cold."

The sound of horses could be heard and looking down the slope, they saw the three remaining Comanche riding away.

"Wonder why they didn't take our horses?" Wallace asked

"Too busy getting to their friends. They'll be back with their friends in a couple of hours," Tye said. Looking up the slope, he shouted. "ADAM, those Comanche that just rode off will be back with their friends in an hour or so. We need to move now. You can come with us and have a chance to get out of this alive or stay here and die for sure."

"They are going to hang me for sure if I go with you."

"Did you kill the Ross's?"

"Hell no," Adam shouted back. "I let them idiots talk me into robbing the place and that damn Neuman did the killing. No one was supposed to get hurt."

"Was he the one that drew his gun at the crossing?"

"Yes…he was a crazy bastard. I've regretted what happened every minute of the day and night since then. Mrs. Ross was good to me."

"We're leaving, Adam. You saved Wallace's life. That will go good for you, and I can speak for you too. You might just get off with a prison sentence. You stay here, you're going to die."

Wallace and Tye started down the slope. Reaching the bottom where the horses were, a lot of noise coming from above them got their attention. Looking up, they saw Adam coming down. Tye smiled. He walked over to get the dead Comanche's pony for Adam to ride.

The two were sitting on their horses when Adam reached level ground. The outlaw had his rifle in his hand, his finger on the trigger and the barrel resting in his left hand. It was not pointed directly at the two men but close enough to make a person nervous. He walked past Tye and up to Wallace. Tye suspected Wallace was not as anxious to kill Adam as he was thirty minutes ago. Wallace sat there, not knowing what the young man was up to..

"Here," Adam said, handing Wallace his rifle and then his Colt revolver. Tye would laugh about it later. A few minutes ago, Wallace wanted to kill the 'bastard,' as he called Adam, and now, the man was handing him his guns. The old cowboy didn't know what to make of it. This 'bastard' had saved his life. He handed the guns back to Adam.

"You keep them for awhile. You'll probably need them pretty damn quick."

"Can you ride bareback?" Tye asked. Adam didn't answer as he jumped on the Indian pony's back and the three of them galloped southeast. Southeast would not take them directly back to Fort Clark, but more toward Fort Inge. Heading directly toward Clark would take them into the path of the Comanche he was sure were coming back. Going in the direction they were headed would lead to the Old Mail Road just west of Fort Inge, forty or so miles east of Brackettville and Fort Clark. They galloped the horses for a couple of miles and then slowed to a canter, then finally, a fifteen minute walk. They followed this routine for an hour and a half before reining their mounts to a halt. Dismounting, each man poured a little water from the canteens into their hats for the horses. Tye commented there would be no camp tonight. He said that to keep moving was their only chance to stay ahead of the Comanche. Tye thought if they could make it till morning, they would be close enough to Inge that the Indians might not want to risk running into a patrol. It was now mid-afternoon and it would be a long time till daylight tomorrow. Tye's main concern was the horses holding up. He was sure Sandy would and probably Wallace's, but the Indian pony was a question mark. The pony looked strong now, but there were a lot of miles to cover, and Indian mounts were not noted for their endurance.

Chapter Eleven

"What river is this?" Wallace asked as they sat on their horses on the bank of a wide, shallow river.

"I'm not sure," Tye answered. "If I was guessing, I would say the West Nueces. I'm not familiar with this part of the country, but if I'm right, this river could be a life saver for us."

"How's that?" Adam asked.

"It's hard to read tracks under the water. We can follow it staying in the water all the way to the Old Mail Road and then follow the road west toward Fort Clark. We can't travel as fast, but at the same time, it will slow the Comanche down some while running up and down both sides of the river trying to find our tracks coming out."

Tye dismounted and took his canteen and kneeling, begin filling it from the river.

"Water doesn't look to good," Wallace commented.

"If you get thirsty enough, it will," Tye chuckled. The two men filled theirs, before allowing the horses to drink their fill. Adam looked back where they had come from.

"Do you think they are coming?"

"They're coming," Tye answered. "Maybe not all of them, but I figure at least twenty or so. We killed one of their friends and embarrassed another. The Comanche, like the Apache, are a proud people. They will want revenge."

The three men mounted their horses, staying in the edge of the river, heading southeast. The water was only six inches deep, but it was flowing and would wash away their tracks quickly.

Tye commented, "This stream, if it is the Nueces, used to be considered the boundary between Texas and Mexico."

"I thought the boundary was always the Rio Grande," Wallace said.

"Nope, that's what most people think. If you look back in history, Mexico claimed all the land west of this river since before and a little after the Texas Revolution. Texas declared the Rio Grande as the border according to the Treaty of Velasco signed by Santa Anna after he got his butt whipped at the Battle of San Jacinto. This boundary disagreement led to the Mexican-American war.

"I didn't know the Mexicans claimed this land," Wallace said looking back over his shoulder for Comanche.

"Until we took it from them...right?" Adam said

"Yep!" Tye said. "Until we took it from them, just like we are doing to the Indians now."

"You consider this land the Indians," Wallace asked?

Tye waited for a few seconds before replying. "I don't know. They have been here a long time. If I was an Indian and my father and my father's father had been here their entire lives, I would probably consider it my land. That's what the whole Indian problem is about. They are fighting for the land, to preserve their way of life, but I'll leave the why's and wherefore's to the politicians."

After splashing through the shallow river for two hours Tye called a halt to let the horses rest a few minutes. A hill, higher than any of the others around, was about a quarter mile to their right. Tye sat there looking and wondering if he should ride over there. From the top he might be able to see their back trail for quite a ways. He'd like to know how much of a lead they had over the Comanche.

He walked around Sandy, looking him over. He still appeared strong and ready to go.

"He probably knows we are headed home and he's anxious to get in the stables and some of that good grain." He smiled, patted Sandy on the neck and stepped into the saddle.

"You two stay here till I get back. I'm going up there," he said nodding to the tall hill. "We need to know if they are back there and how much of a lead we have. I won't be gone more than fifteen minutes."

It only took a couple minutes for Sandy to gallop to the base of the hill and another couple to get close to the top. Tye reined him in and stepped from the saddle before reaching the summit. He crouched and made his way the last few feet to the crest. Not wanting to be sky lined, he stayed below the tops of the cedar and sage that covered the hill. Using his binoculars he quickly scanned both sides of the river. The terrain along the river was flat and he estimated he could see five miles. The only movement he saw was a small herd of antelope heading toward the river for their evening drink. He moved the binoculars away from the river and looked at the low hills that the river ran through. He saw nothing there either. He sat there for a couple more minutes.

"Maybe I was wrong and they are not coming," he thought. He started to go back down the hill to Sandy, but decided to take one more look. Raising the binoculars, the first thing he saw was the herd of antelope he had seen earlier. The antelope were running away from the river this time. He looked a little farther upstream and saw them-twenty or so Comanche. They were split into two groups, one on each side of the river. Like he thought earlier, they were moving pretty slow, looking for tracks. He figured the three of them had about an hour lead. He hurried down the hill, mounted Sandy and headed back where Wallace and Adam waited.

"See anything?" Adam asked.

"Yeah, I saw a lot of Comanche…twenty or twenty-five of them. They're about an hour behind us."

Wallace and Adam mounted their horses. Wallace looked over his shoulder in the direction the Indians would be coming.

"What's the plan?"

"Keep moving like we are and try to keep the same distance between us. It'll be dark in a couple hours. There won't be a moon tonight so I figure they will stay on the trail until full dark. It will be too dark to see tracks leaving the river, so they'll probably make camp. If they think like the Apache, they'll believe we will make camp like all white men do every night on the trail. If we keep moving, we can increase our lead. With luck, we should be close to Fort Inge by daylight."

~~

Two Moons held up his hand and the warriors with him gathered around. The braves on the other side of the river led their ponies through the shallow water to where he sat on his horse. Two Moons was a warrior of great status among his people. That is the reason his chief, Crooked Nose, had sent him back to find the white men and kill them.

When all the braves had gathered around him he spoke.

"The sun will be gone soon. I will take Little Wolf, Two Feathers, and Spotted Horse with me. We are going to try to catch up with the white men. I think they will stay in the water which slows them down. We will run our ponies on the dry land. The rest of you stay on the banks and make sure we don't miss their tracks leaving the water. If we find them, I will send Spotted Horse back to you. When it becomes too dark to see, make camp but be ready to leave quickly." He looked at the three warriors he had named and said, "Let us find the white-eyes."

Out of the river and on the fairly flat land, Two Moons let his pony run free. The wind in his face felt cool, his long raven hair with the eagle feather blowing in the wind. He was tall, muscular, and if he had been born a white man, would be considered handsome by the ladies. He had counted many coups against the blue coats and the Kiowa. He was fearless in battle like all Comanche, but what set him apart from the others was his cunning and leadership. The other warriors looked to him in times of trouble. That is why he was selected as their war chief and if their chief, Crooked Nose was killed, he would be Chief of all the Comanche.

He and his pony were as one as they raced along the flat land that bordered the river. Like all Comanche, he spent a lot of time astride his ponies. No other tribe had the reputation the Comanche had as being good horsemen. He intended to catch up with the white men before dark even if he had to run his pony into the ground. He thought they would stay in the river which would slow them down considerably.

Just when he thought his pony was beginning to reach the limit of his endurance, he spotted the white men no more than three hundred yards ahead of him. He knew the Great Spirit smiled on him because at this particular place on the river were the only rapids he knew of, and the white men, being in the water along the bank, could not hear their pony's hoof beats. He slowed his pony, as did the others and spread out in a line where all could shoot the repeating rifles they had taken from the Kiowa. Advancing toward the white men at a trot, they were no more than sixty or seventy yards from the men when he saw one look back and apparently shouted a warning because the other two looked back. Two Moons reined his pony in as did the others and quickly each raised their rifles and fired.

Adam. Looking over his shoulder screamed.

"COMANCHE...THE COMANCHE ARE BEHIND US."

Tye and Wallace's heads snapped around and all three men had their horses out of the water and running the next second. They heard the rifles firing, and Tye heard a grunt and a curse from Wallace as he slumped over his saddle. Tye reached back, grabbing the wounded man by the collar and held him in the saddle as they rode hell-bent-for-leather along the rocky ground. He glanced over his shoulder and saw the smoke from the rifles as the Indians fired again. As he watched, he saw them kicking their ponies into a run to catch up. He glanced at Wallace and saw the hole and blood in his shoulder. He was hit hard.

The initial shock of being hit was past and Wallace sat upright in the saddle and pushed Tye's hand away giving the scout a thank you nod for keeping him in the saddle. Tye knew he had to be feeling a hell of lot of pain. He knew all too well how much a bullet could hurt having being shot more than once himself. He also knew that Wallace could not stay in the saddle long, because he was losing a lot of blood and soon would be too weak and dizzy. Tye began looking for a place to fort up. Looking along the hills to his right, he saw the perfect place. He reined Sandy to the right and the others followed. The slope was steep but along the top was a vertical cliff twenty feet or so high. He headed toward a small cave he had spotted in the face of the cliff. The horses were struggling in the loose rock so Tye jumped off Sandy, as did Adam.

"Take Wallace and the horses to that cave," he said pointing with his Henry he had jerked from the saddle scabbard. He handed Adam his and Wallace's reins. Tye turned, facing down the slope. The Comanche's horses had apparently reached their limits of endurance sometime in the chase because they had fallen back a hundred yards. Kneeling, he raised the rifle to his shoulder, and squeezed off a round. The rifle bucked slightly against his shoulder and he saw a horse stumble and fall, throwing its rider to the ground. He fired again and one of the warriors somersaulted off the back of his pony, hit the ground and did not move. The other's veered to the left, down the slope and out of range of the Henry.

Two Moons saw the unmoving body of his friend, Spotted Horse. He spat in disgust.

"The white man in the deer-skin shirt will die a thousand deaths for killing my friend, "he promised himself. The sun was setting behind the hills and darkness would be on them quickly. "Little Wolf, make your way back and find the rest and bring them here." He turned to Two Feathers. "You and I will keep the white men in that cave until Little Wolf returns with the others."

Tye entered the cave and looked at Wallace grimacing in pain. Tye, kneeling, unbuttoned Wallace's shirt so he could look at the wound.

"Damn," he thought. *"No exit wound means more pain for the man when the bullet is dug out. That's going to have to wait for awhile though. I've got to get a plan together to get us out of this mess."* He looked at Adam.

"I like the man, but could I trust him to stay here with Wallace while I went for help? If we stay here we can hold them

for awhile, but eventually, lack of water or running out of bullets will do us in."

"Adam, we have two choices: we can stay here and eventually be killed or one of us can make a run for help. How much do you weigh, one hundred and forty or so?" Adam nodded. "Sandy is used to my two hundred so you will be like a fly on his back."

"What are you getting at?"

"I want you to take Sandy and Wallace's horse and ride for help. You can change mounts every few minutes to keep them fresh. I noticed the Comanche's ponies were used up so if you get going before the others get back, they will never catch you."

"I...I don't think I could find anyone to help. I'm not sure I can find the fort. Adam commented.

"All you have to do is follow the river till you get to the Old Mail Road. Go east and you will run into Fort Inge. They know me there. There is a certain lieutenant by the name of Rogers. Ask for him. Now, we don't have much time so let's do it. Do you have any spare cartridges?"

Adam took a handful from his pocket and a dozen out of the loops on his belt, and
handed them to Tye. Tye took a box from his saddle bag and rummaged through Wallace's and found another one. Standing up he grabbed Sandy's reins and handed the other reins to Adam.

"Let's go and be damn quite." They led the horses from the cave. It had become quite dark as they walked along the bottom of the cliff. Both men held the reins in one hand and kept the other hand over their horse's nostrils to keep them from snorting or whinnying. Considering everything, Tye thought they were being exceptionally quite. They walked for more than a hundred yards before Tye signaled them to stop. I'm going back to the cave." He handed Sandy's reins to Adam. He stroked Sandy's neck and told Adam to step in the saddle. He knew Sandy did not like strangers so Tye was sweet talking him while Adam adjusted his butt in the saddle. "Walk them at least another hundred yards Adam, then ease them down the slope. When you hit flat ground give Sandy free rein and let him pick his way. Keep them at a gallop and stay with the river."

Adam nodded and looked at Tye.

"I know you think I am a bad person and probably cannot be trusted, but I will be back...I swear to you."

Tye smiled and patted the man on the knee. "If I didn't think you would, I wouldn't send you. Now get going and be careful." Tye made his way back to the cave being extremely careful of not making any noise. When he arrived he whispered, "Wallace...it's me, Tye. Don't shoot."

"Come on," Wallace replied. After sitting down on the rocky floor of the cave, Tye looked at Wallace. The man's black beard was wet with sweat and beads could be seen on his forehead and dripping from his nose. Tye knew the man was hurting something terrible.

"Wallace, the only way you are going to feel better is to let me get that bullet out. It's going to hurt like hell, but it's only going to get worse if we don't get it out."

Wallace looked at Tye. "I suppose you have done this before?"

Tye smiled. "More than once."

"How bad?"

"How bad what?" Tye asked.

"Hell, man, how bad is it going to hurt to get the damn thing out?"

"It's going to hurt, Wallace, no way around that, but in the end, it's the only way it will quit hurting and besides, if the lead does not come out, you could die."

"Hell of a choice ain't it," he spat. He rolled over on his right side so Tye could get to the wound. "Let's get it over with." Twenty minutes later it was over. Fortunately for Wallace, he had passed out while Tye was probing for the lead. Tye bandaged the wound as best he could with Wallace's sleeve from the man's long johns.

Moving over to the mouth of the cave, Tye listened. No sound could be heard. He scooted a little farther and looking down, saw three fires indicating the rest of the Comanche's had arrived. He scooted back inside the cave.

"Things are going to get pretty hot here at daylight," he thought. *"I hope Wallace comes around. If he does, being hit in the left shoulder will allow him to use his gun with his right. He moved back to the mouth of the cave and looked at the stars to see what time it was. He figured it's close to midnight. That would mean Adam has been gone about three hours. He should be getting close to the Mail Road."* He took one more look out the cave and then moved back and sat with his back to the wall. He took a deep breath, exhaling slowly. *It's going to be a long night,* he thought. As usual, at night when he was on scout, his thoughts drifted back to Rebecca and here lately, the fact he was about to become a father.

" I'm lucky to have a friend like Buff to take care of her when I'm not there and she is so fortunate to have the O'Malley's. They are like parents to her. Mrs. O'Malley, she frets more over Rebecca than any woman he had seen fret over anything. Rebecca could not be in better hands and I'm thankful for that." He shut his eyes. *"I'm in the worst position I have been in for a long time and if Adam doesn't make it back soon...."* The thought brought a lump to his throat, not that he was afraid of dying because he wasn't. He believed in God and life after death and by dying he

would live again. The thought of leaving Rebecca and never seeing his baby ripped his heart out.

A slight noise came from just outside the cave and he was immediately alert, his Henry pointed at the opening of the cave. He listened for any other sound, but heard nothing. He almost believed he had imagined the sound when he heard something like cloth scraping. He slid his butt a couple feet farther into the cave, never taking his eyes or the barrel of his Henry away from the opening. They were coming.

~~

Adam sat on Sandy about two hundred yards from the campfire he had spotted. After watching the camp for five minutes he could not decide who were camped there-white men or Indians. There were two small fires and he could see shadowy figures moving around the camp, but he was too far away and it was to dark to tell who or what the men were.

"I've got to find out and I need to know now." He dismounted and tied the reins of Sandy and the other horse to the branch of a mesquite. With his Colt in his right hand, he moved slowly toward the fire. Sixty yards out he heard what sounded like laughter and then he saw a blue clad soldier walk in the light of the fire. Excitement filled him as he shouted.

"HELLO THE CAMP." Immediately he saw a number of men scrambling around the camp. From Adam's right, a voice startled him.

"WHO GOES THERE?"

Adam was surprised he had not seen the guard and the guard had not seen him. *"Damn guard must have been dozing and my voice probably scared the hell out of him."* He hollered his name and it was followed by a voice from the camp. "Come in slowly."

"Let me get my horses," Adam replied. Adam holstered his gun and walked back to the horses and then toward the camp. An officer and two enlisted men met him at the edge of the camp.

The officer spoke. "I'm Captain Ackerley. May I ask what you are doing roaming around this country at night?"

"Are you from Fort Inge?"

"Yes sir. We're on patrol from Inge," the officer said. Another officer, a lieutenant, came up to them and he was paying a lot of attention to Sandy.

"Where did you get this horse?" the lieutenant demanded seeing the U.S. Army brand. The captain looked at the lieutenant.

"Why do you ask the man that?"

"I know this horse, Sir. It belongs to Tye Watkins, the scout at Fort Clark." The captain's head jerked back, his eyes burning into Adam's.

"That right...is this Watkins horse?"

Adam nodded. "It's Sandy, Tye's horse. We..."

He did not finish as the Captain interrupted him. "You had better tell me how you acquired this horse and damn quick and you had better make me believe your story."

"Do you know a Lieutenant Rogers?"

"Why do you ask?"

"Tye told me to ask for him."

"I'm Lieutenant Rogers," the young Lieutenant said stepping forward.

Adam told the whole story of what had happened...all except about the robbery. He figured that would come out later.

"Tye's in a fix and needs some help. He could have gotten away but stayed with Wallace."

"That's what Tye would do alright," Rogers said. He turned to the captain. "We need to get there with all haste, Sir."

Ackerley turned to Sergeant Jackson. "Get the patrol mounted and prepared to move out Sergeant." He turned back to Adam. "Can you find where the men are holed up in the dark?" Adam nodded. The captain looked at the two horses. "Do you think they will carry you back?"

Adam nodded again. "I've been switching back and forth. They can make it okay." Five minutes later the patrol moved out and headed north, following the Nueces and Adam.

Second Chance

~~

Back at Fort Clark the vigil over Todd continued. Sergeant O'Malley was by his bed tonight and would be until Sergeant Christian relieved him in an hour or so. Todd had showed signs of regaining consciousnesses a couple of times during the day, but so far, had not. Buff said while he was there earlier, Todd's eyes had fluttered like he was waking up, but then they stopped and he remained like he was.

Major Thurston checked in several times. He had made inquires about who might have been responsible for Todd's injuries, but so far had come up empty. The only chance they had of finding out who did it was Todd. He could identify the man and they would find him if they had to search the whole damn country.

Rebecca was holding up well with all that was going on: Todd injured, Tye gone, and her expecting a child shortly. So far, she had had no complications and very little sickness. Mrs. O'Malley had seen that she had not needed anything. She had organized the ladies at the fort to make clothes and bedding for the baby. Everything was in its' place and ready for the big event except one, Tye. Rebecca prayed every night when she went to bed and again when she woke up that he would be okay and would return to her like he always had before.

Chapter Twelve

Tye was surprised the Comanche were coming at night. He wasn't as familiar with them as he was with the Apache, but he knew most Indians did not like fighting at night fearing that if killed, their spirit would wander in darkness forever. These must not believe that. He had his pistol out, and on the rocky floor of the cave beside him within easy reach. He could hear more of the sight scraping sounds and knew they were close.

"Why wait on them to rush in when I can take the fight to them. Thank God I have a Henry instead of the single shot old Sharps."

He stood up, as much as he could anyway since the cave was only five feet or so high, and rushed to the opening. He fired his Henry as fast as he could work the lever and pull the trigger. Not aiming at anything in particular, he swept the area in front of the cave firing until the hammer fell on an empty chamber. He reached down and grabbed his pistol and was ready to fire it but did not hear or see anything. Sitting down, he listened. The only sound was his beating heart. He reloaded the Henry and waited, listening. A sound reached his ear, but he couldn't figure out what it was. It was a continuous sound and then after a minute, stopped and then there was nothing. It sounded like a groan.   .

He scooted over to the opening and looked down the slope. There was a lot of activity below in the camp. The fires were blazing and a lot of whooping and hollering was going on.

"My firing all those shots must have done some damage because they are sure as hell riled up." As he watched, the shouting stopped, and everyone sat down except one warrior who was talking to them. It made no difference that Tye could not hear his words because he knew very little Comanche. The man was quite demonstrative though, waving his arms as he talked and every once in awhile raising his voice loud enough for Tye to hear his words. Tye looking over the rest of the camp, saw what he figured was the reason for the noise and the speech by whoever the warrior was. Three bodies lay on the edge of the firelight and another warrior was sitting, holding his shoulder.

A moan behind him followed by a couple of curses indicated Wallace was awake. "You okay Wallace?" he asked.

"That's the stupidest damn question I've heard in my whole miserable life," he replied. Tye could barely make out his face in the dark but he could see enough to see the misery etched in it. "You ask me how I feel!" he said in a high pitched voice. "You know damn well how I feel. It hurts every time my damn heart beats."

Tye laughed and said, "That's a good thing."

"I just thought that remark a minute ago was the stupidest remark I ever heard, but you just topped it with that one," Wallace said, then grimaced as a new wave of pain swept over him. "Damn!"

"Listen Wallace. I know you are hurting, but what I meant by that remark is that you could be dead and not feeling anything. At least you're alive."

Wallace tried to laugh, but failed. "I guess you're right, but damn, when the pain gets bad…I wonder."

Tye smiled. "You get a little sleep because I am going to need you around daylight. We have a lot of Comanche down the slope and they're going to pay us a visit about the time the sun comes up." Wallace nodded and then grimaced again.

"Did you do some shooting awhile ago?"

Tye nodded his head. "Yeah. A few of them tried to sneak in. I don't think they will try it again. They will wait till daylight and rush us all at once."

"I must have been out of it. I heard the shooting, but it seemed like a dream."

"I assure you Wallace, this is no dream. Now get some rest." Tye moved back to the opening and listened. There was no sound, no sign of anyone close to the cave. He sat down and leaned back against the cave wall and allowing his senses to become accustomed to the natural sounds of the night: the fluttering of bats searching for a night time meal, the scratching of claws as a small lizard ran across the floor of the cave, the night-time breeze rustling the leaves of the mesquite. By becoming tuned to these natural sounds, he could doze off, and any unnatural sound would wake him immediately. This was a trick he learned from his pa. Over the years he had known a lot of fighting men who used this method when they needed some rest. He made sure his Henry was cocked, breathed deep and exhaled slowly, relaxed, and shut his eyes.

Tye woke up suddenly, and it took him a second or two to remember where he was. Wondering what had woke him up so abruptly he was startled to see the gray of pre dawn outside the cave. He realized there was a lot of noise from below in the Comanche camp. He looked out and they were spreading out all along the base of the hill and he knew they were preparing to come. He reached over and shook Wallace awake. "It's time Wallace. See if you can move over here where you can help me." With some moaning and cursing, Wallace was beside Tye with his pistol in his right hand.

"Let the red devils come and get some of this," he said holding the pistol up and waving it at the Comanche gathering at the base of the hill. Tye smiled. He liked this man.

"I think he could face the devil himself and not be afraid," he thought. Tye thought they had a good chance of holding them off for awhile, at least till Adam returned. They had some cover and the cave was deep enough that he didn't think bullets ricocheting would be a problem. With a little luck they just might kill enough of them they might consider the white men not worth it and leave. He doubted that though.

He gave Wallace his pistol and he had Wallace's Henry. Between the two Henry's and two pistols, they could fire close to forty times before reloading. They could do a lot of damage with that many rounds.

Screams broke the stillness as they came up the slope toward the cave. Tye leveled the rifle at the one leading the charge and squeezed the trigger. The warrior, hit in the chest, was propelled backwards, knocking the man behind him down. Tye moved the barrel slightly to the right and fired again. Another brave was taken out of the charge. Wallace was firing now and Tye saw a couple of Comanche go down. The Comanche learned quickly and changed tactics. They would all charge a couple of steps and then quickly hit the slope on their bellies. They would crawl a few feet, jump up and charge two or three steps, hit the slope again, never giving a man time to line one up in his sights.

The white men knew they would be overrun at the rate the Comanche were gaining ground in ten or fifteen minutes. The only way they could fire at the prone warriors was to scoot farther toward the opening and this would expose them to fire.

"*If the soldiers don't show up in a minute it will be all over.*" A lump formed in Tye's throat at the thought of Rebecca and never seeing his child, never holding his and Rebecca's baby. He swallowed and shook that thought from his head.

"*I'm going to live dammit! I am going to live and the only way is to stop them from over running us.*" He crawled to the edge of the slope and started firing as fast as he could. He swept the barrel from left to right and back again. Bullets smashed against the cave walls, and whistled as they ricocheted back into the cave. It was total chaos for a few seconds, but Tye's rapid firing on them had forced the Indians to halt their advance. In his wild firing he had hit three of them, killing one and wounding two. He scooted back into the cave beside Wallace.

"That was a damn fool thing to do!" Wallace shouted.

"I had to do something. The way they were coming they would have been all over us in minutes."

Less than a mile away, the firing could be heard by Adam and the patrol. The men formed a skirmish line with Ackerley and

James in the middle, along with Adam. The soldier's horses went from a canter to a gallop. When they could see the Comanche they went into an all out charge. The Comanche, who were more than half way up the slope, saw the troopers charging, turned and went rushing down the slope to get to the pony herd. They did not make it. The troopers were on them and it was close in, hand to hand fighting. Tye scrambled down the slope, wanting to help. He watched one Comanche jump on the rear of a trooper's horse stabbing the rider several times in the back. He threw the dead soldier from the saddle and raced away. Tye stopped, took aim and knocked the warrior from the horse. The fight lasted no more than a minute and it was over. Seven Comanche warriors stood with their hands in the air. The rest were dead.

Tye saw three troopers lying among the dead Comanche. Adam rode Sandy to where he stood. The two shook hands. "I knew you would be back," Tye said.

A big smile spread across Adam's young face. "I didn't know if we would be here in time or not."

Tye turned toward a familiar voice coming from behind him. "Well, how does it feel to have your butt pulled out of the fire for a change?"

"Lieutenants Rogers. I'll be damned." Tye said when he saw the blond hair under the hat. "I see you haven't lost that yellow hair yet."

Rogers laughed. "Not yet, but I'm considering changing the color." The captain rode over to them. "Tye, I would like you to meet Captain Ackerley. Captain, this is Tye Watkins from Fort Clark."

"My pleasure Captain."

"The pleasure's mine. From all the stories I have heard, plus this here Lieutenant talking about you, I thought you would be eight foot tall." He laughed.

"I don't know what all you have heard, but you know how stories become…a little stretched from actual events. It's a pleasure to meet you, and good to see this here young Lieutenant again." He looked around. "Your timing was good, Captain."

"You can thank that young cowboy over there," Ackerley said.

"I intend to do just that. By the way, up north a ways we saw the main bunch that these came from. There's probably still over fifty of them running loose."

"As soon as we clean up this mess," the captain said sweeping his arm over the battlefield, "We'll see if we can pick up the tracks."

"I hope you can, and keep them up here. We sure as hell don't need them farther west to go along with our Apache problems at Clark. The Apache are more than a handful as it is."

He started back up the hill to check on Wallace while the soldiers cleaned up the area and took care of their dead and wounded. Arriving at the cave, he saw Adam giving Wallace some water from his canteen.

"How's the water, Wallace?" Tye asked.

"Like you said yesterday, if you get thirsty enough… it's damn good."

Tye looked at Adam. "I want to thank you for what you did Adam. You could have kept on going and no one would have known any different. You would have been free."

"Yes, I would have been, but I would always be looking over my shoulder, always wondering if the stranger coming down the road was looking for me. I am not a murderer, Tye. I made a mistake, and I guess I'll take my chances with the law."

"I intend to speak on your behalf." Tye put his hand on the young man's shoulder. "That's a promise."

Wallace painfully got to his feet. He stuck out his hand to Adam. "No one hated you more than me for what happened at the Rocking B." Adam took his hand and Wallace looked him in the eye. "I will stand by Tye and help you anyway I can."

Adam choked back his emotion and simply said, "Thanks, Wallace."

Tye spoke up. "You saved our hides, Adam. That should be good for something in court."

"We'll see," Adam said. Tye and Adam helped the wounded Wallace down the slope to where Captain Ackerley and Lieutenant Rogers waited. Reaching level ground where the two officers waited, Tye introduced Wallace to the both of them. After the handshakes, the captain looked at Tye.

"We're ready to move out. I would appreciate you helping Private Jacobs over there find his way back to Inge with our dead and wounded."

Tye nodded. "Do I need to go to Inge and report what happened here to your commanding officer?"

Ackerley shook his head. "Private Jacobs has a dispatch filling him in. I asked him to send another patrol to catch up and reinforce us."

Tye looked at the patrol that was formed and ready to go. "Be careful you don't catch up to them before help arrives, Sir. They have you outnumbered by better than two to one. As you know with Indians, that is a sure bet on having a massacre."

"I understand that very well and we'll be careful."

Tye shook both men's hand, and thanked them again. Of course, Rogers had the last word as they rode off.

"Feel's good to have your butt pulled out of the fire doesn't it Tye?" He laughed at the remark. His butt had been saved by Tye from an Apache ambush about a year ago.

The three of them stood watching the patrol ride off. After a minute, Tye turned to Private Jacobs. "You ready to ride?"

"Yes, Sir." Each body had been wrapped in a blanket and tied across the saddle of a horse. The wounded were all able to ride except the three critically wounded. Tye made a travois for each of them to be pulled behind a horse. It would slow them down some but it would be a hell of a lot more comfortable for the three men. Fifteen minutes after the patrol left, the three men along with the private and the dead and wounded headed south. The seven captured warriors walked ahead of the men, hands tied behind their backs, a rope around each of their necks and tied to the one on front of him. They walked in single file with four feet of rope between each.

Chapter Thirteen

It was mid-afternoon when the little group arrived at The Old Mail Road. Tye was afraid what might happen with the private guarding seven warriors with his single shot Sharps while making his way to Inge. He took another piece of rope and tied one leg of each warrior to it. He then gave the private one of the Henrys they had taken from the Comanche. With their legs tied the way they were, it would be impossible for them to rush the young private without stumbling and taking each other down. It was only a few miles and he figured the young soldier would be fine.

"Make sure you stay a good distance behind them and don't take your eyes off them. If they make any kind of move…shoot to kill. If that happens and you have to kill one or two, don't cut the ropes…make the others carry them. You get close enough to them to cut the ropes they'll jump you. Understood? "

"Yes Sir."

Wallace, Adam, and he headed west, toward Fort Clark. Tye figured they could make it by midnight. He was anxious to see Rebecca and make sure everything was okay with her. Wallace was anxious to see how his boss of the Rocking B and his friend, Lester were, and to see how their wounds were coming along. His shoulder was feeling better since the surgeon with the patrol had doctored his wounds before they parted company. Adam wasn't as anxious to get to the fort. He knew a cell was waiting for him... and maybe the hangman.

There was little talk as the three men rode, alternating between walking and galloping their mounts. For Tye and Wallace, they were glad to be alive, and Adam hoped he had proved that he wasn't a bad guy, just one who made a bad decision. He wondered if that decision was going to ruin his whole life...or end it. It would kill his folks when they found out he was in prison or worse, hung for murder. He could not believe he had been such a fool, but he was now determined to face whatever his actions warranted.

Wallace wanted to get back to the Rocking B and the life of a cowboy. This life of chasing outlaws and fighting Indians wasn't for him. He was a cowboy and was content to ride for his boss's brand for thirty-five dollars a month. He had a good breakfast every morning and a good evening meal every night, plus a roof over his head. What more could a man who wanted nothing more in life than to be a cowboy, want.

The sun was setting in front of them when they passed a spot on the Old Mail Road Tye would never forget. Eighteen or so months ago, he had been dispatched to find an overdue pay wagon. It was here where he had found the wagon and what was left of the detail that was guarding it. They had been executed by the Vazquez gang and left for the buzzards that did quite a job of ripping the bodies apart.

~~

The doctor at Clark checked Todd's vitals. A few minutes earlier, Buff, who was taking his turn sitting with Todd, noticed a change. Todd began moving his feet and hands and mumbling words that Buff could not understand. Buff immediately summoned the doc to see what was going on. He also sent for Sergeant O'Malley.

When the old sergeant arrived the doc was still examining Todd.

"What's going on, Buff?"

"Todd began moving his hands and feet and mumbling, but I couldn't understand what he was saying, so I sent for the Doc and you." The doc came over to the two men.

He had a smile on his face. "His vitals are good and his moving his hands, feet and trying to talk is a good sign that he may be beginning to regain consciousness.

"How soon?" Buff asked.

The surgeon scratched the back of his neck. "Hard to say Buff. It could be in the next breath, or in a few hours, but he's going to come around. I really think he will be fine."
He walked away from the bed leaving Buff and O'Malley.

O'Malley spoke. "You go back to the house and keep an eye on Rebecca. I'll stay here for awhile."

Buff nodded. "I'll stop by the enlisted men's quarters on my way and get someone to relieve you in a hour or so."

Tye and the others rode across the bridge into Fort Clark shortly after midnight. They went directly to Tye's home. Tye knew Rebecca would be asleep, so he tapped lightly on the door. He knew the tapping would wake up Buff. In a few seconds, he heard Buff whisper.

"Who's there?"

"Buff, it's me, Tye." The door opened slightly and the first thing out the door was the muzzle of a rifle.

"By God! It is you, Tye." The barrel lowered and Buff stepped out and stuck out his hand and taking Tye's hand, pumping it heartily.

"How's Rebecca?"

"She's fine. No problems other than missing you," he said laughing. He noticed the other two men. He knew Wallace, having met him when he brought his wounded boss and friend in to the hospital. "Good to see you Wallace," he said shaking the man's hand.

"Good to see you again, Buff." Tye looked at Adam.

"Buff, this young man here is Adam Carter." Buff stepped back.

"The man you were chasing," he questioned? Buff was confused, seeing the man had a gun on his hip.

Adam, noticing Buff looking at his gun and began unbuckling the belt. "I guess I won't need this for awhile."

"Keep your gun for now," Tye said.

"What's going on Tye?"

Tye smiled. "It's a long story, Buff. I'll explain later."

"What's going on, Buff," Rebecca asked from the bedroom?

Tye put his finger to his lips signaling Buff not to say anything. "I'm going to surprise Rebecca," he whispered. He looked at Wallace and Adam. "I'll be out in a minute."

Nothing was said for a few seconds between the three men before Wallace spoke up. "Buff, do you know how Mr. Ross and Lester are doing?"

"Lester is staying in Tye's old quarters and Mr. Ross is still in the hospital. Doc says he is doing fine."

Tye came out of the room with Rebecca. "Rebecca just told me about Todd. We're going to the hospital now. Adam, make you a bed on the floor by the fireplace. Buff can show you where the blankets are." He turned to Wallace. "Lester is staying in my old quarters. It's on the way to the hospital so I'll show you where it is. There's room for you there, and you can fill in your partner on what has happened the last couple days." Lester nodded, and the three of them left the house, leaving Buff and Adam.

After dropping Wallace off they had made their way to the hospital. Sergeant Arnold, who had relieved O'Malley, was in the room sitting with the boy. He stood up from the chair and shook Tye's hand and tipped his hat to Rebecca. He walked outside to give Rebecca and Tye a little privacy with Todd. Tye was shocked at the sight…his swollen and bruised face startled him. If he did not know it was Todd, he would have never recognized him. The initial shock went away and anger rose inside of him, an anger that started at his very core and worked its way up. Rebecca noticed it immediately.

"He's going to be okay, Honey," Rebecca said, trying to calm him. "The doctor said he thought he would be fine. It's just going to take time.

"I'm going to kill him, Rebecca. I'm going to find the bastard that done this, and I'm gonna kill him." She saw his hands gripping the back of the chair and his knuckles were white from squeezing the chair. "I swear… he's a dead man."

She wrapped her arms around her man. She had never seen him like this-this mad, almost out-of-control mad. She hugged him tight and could feel him trembling. She was scared, not for herself or for Tye, but for what she was afraid he was about to do. "Honey, calm down. Todd will be fine and then we'll worry about who did this to him." She pulled his head down with her hand so their faces were almost touching. "It's alright Tye. Everything will be alright." She kissed him and he put his arms around her, hugging her tight.

"Not to tight, Tye. We're not alone you know," she said patting her stomach. He stepped back and smiled-not a big smile, but a smile. She could see some of the tension leave him, but she knew it was only temporary.

After talking to Christian for a moment, they headed back to their home. Christian had told them Todd was going to wake up soon. He told Tye that Todd had mumbled some earlier when Buff was here, and had a few times since he had been sitting here. Doc said it was only a matter of time.

Rebecca felt a deep fear, not a fear of something happening to her or the baby, but a fear for Tye. She had seen him really mad only once, and that was a year and a half ago. At the Fourth of July dance, he spotted two Mexicans that had knocked him out, robbed him, and left him for dead. He almost beat the two to death. The anger she saw in him that night didn't compare to the anger she saw in him a few minutes ago. He was a gentle, loving man and it always amazed her how gentle he could be with her, but there was the other side, a side that could terrify her at times when she thought about it. She had been told stories by O'Malley and others on the fort about his ability to be as vicious as the outlaws he chased, or as cruel as the Apache he fought. He could be your best friend and would do anything for you, even die to protect you. He could also become your worst nightmare. The look on his face and his demeanor a few minutes ago told her he was going to become the latter for someone.

Buff met them at the door and stepped out on the porch. "Adam's already asleep. I don't think I ever saw anyone go to sleep that fast."

Tye smiled. "You might want to watch me then. Sleep has been hard to come by lately. I don't think I'll have any trouble tonight."

Buff looked inside the house where Adam lay in front of the fireplace. "Do I need to stay up and watch him?"

"There is no need for that, Buff. He could have run off a dozen times the last two days, but he hasn't. He's not a bad guy, just a young man that got involved with the wrong people and made a bad decision. We'll talk tomorrow, but I will tell you and Rebecca this, if it wasn't for him, Wallace's and my scalp would be hanging on a Comanche's lance right now." Tye walked in the house, pulled his sweat stained buckskin shirt off, and washed his face and hands in the wash basin. "See you in the morning Buff," he whispered. He and Rebecca went into their bedroom.

The morning dawned bright and clear, with a touch of frost on everything. Tye sat up in bed, not believing he had slept this late. He couldn't remember the last time he hadn't awakened long before the sun peeked over the horizon. He quickly dressed and walked out of the bedroom.

"Well, look who decided to finally make an appearance," Buff said, setting down his cup of coffee and leaning back in his chair. "As soon as you get some vittles down, Major Thurston wants you to report to him. Sergeant Christian hobbled over here earlier on his crutches to pass along the message."

Tye, looking out the window, saw Adam standing on the porch with a cup of coffee in his hand. "Where is Rebecca?" He turned his attention away from Adam back to Buff. "You say Christian was here on crutches? What's he doing on crutches? Has anyone heard how Todd is doing this morning?"

"Which damn question would like me to answer first?

"Where's Rebecca?"

"She went to see Todd with Mrs. O'Malley. They should be back soon, and we'll know how he is. As far as Christian is concerned, he broke his leg when his horse was shot. It fell on him three days ago during a fight with some Apache."

Tye nodded, remembering Thurston telling him of a report of some trouble. Sergeant Christian was a good friend of Tye's and was a hell of a soldier. "Where was the fight at?"

"West of here, just south of the Old Mail Road, about thirty miles as the crow flies. The patrol caught up with the band while they were attacking a homestead and killed all of them except for six or so. We lost some men and had several wounded in the fight. From what I heard, it ended up being a close hand-to-hand fight."

Tye nodded and sat down with his cup of coffee. He took a sip and as usual, winced at the first touch of the hot tin cup burned his lips. Adam walked in and sat down.

"Morning Tye, or should I say, good afternoon," he said smiling.

Tye just smiled. "As soon as I get some of this coffee down, we'll check on Todd and then go see Thurston."

A few minutes later the three men walked into the hospital. They arrived as Mrs. O'Malley was coming out.

"Tye, I was just coming to get you," she said, then blurted out in a loud voice, "Todd's awake and talking."

Tye didn't say a word, but his heart rate went up immediately at the thought of Todd telling him what happened. He rushed to Todd's room to find a tearful Rebecca standing beside the bed holding his hand. Tye walked over and put his hand on the boy's forehead.

"How are you doing, boy?"

"Kinda hungry if you want to know the truth," he said forcing a smile to his bruised and swollen lips.

"I bet we can find you something to eat pretty quick."

"The doctor as already sent for some food," Rebecca said.

"How do you feel," Rebecca asked?

"Kinda beat up," Todd answered quickly, the remark bringing a laugh from everyone.

"The kid has a sense of humor," said Adam, staring at the boy. He had never seen anyone beat up like that and for sure, no kid.

Tye bent over Todd and asked quietly, "Who did this to you, Todd? Did you know him?"

Todd shook his head. "I never saw him before. He was a big man with a black beard that covered his whole face. I think he might have been a trapper, or maybe an ex buffalo hunter. He had a heavy robe on that looked like it was made from a buffalo."

"What about his horse?"

"He rode a black with a white blaze that resembled a streak of lightning starting at his forehead and running down his face. It was a good looking horse. We met on the road and he commented about what a fine looking horse I was riding, then he kicked me out of the saddle. I think it knocked the wind out of me when I hit the ground because I know I was hurting when he grabbed me by the collar and jerked me to my feet. I hit him with a good punch, just like you showed me. I caught him on the cheek and I think it hurt him because he cussed something fierce and then hit me…and hit me. I guess I passed out because the next thing I knew, I'm here with you and Rebecca."

"I'm going to check around, Todd. Right now I have to report to the major." He nodded to Rebecca. "I'll see you in a little while." Buff and Rebecca stayed with Todd. The orderly opened the door to Thurston's office and announced that Tye was here. Tye heard the chair scrape the wooden floor as the major pushed back from the desk and came out to meet him, shaking Tye's hand

"Glad you're back, Tye." Noticing the man with him, he asked. "Is this the…" he hesitated for a second. "Is this the man you were after, Adam Carter?"

Adam stuck out his hand. "Yes Sir, I'm Adam." After hesitating for a couple of seconds, Thurston shook his hand while looking at Tye wondering what was going on. The man Tye was chasing was standing here with a gun strapped on his hip. Tye saw the disturbed look on the major's face.

"We need to talk Major."

Thurston nodded. "Indeed we do. Come on in."

Second Chance

Tye started from the fight at the crossing and explained Adam never fired a shot. He commented on what happened at the Wilson homestead where he could have robbed them, but didn't and even left money for the food they gave him. He told him of the rancher that would have offered him a job, and then about the Comanche fight and how Adam could have run and no one would have ever known the difference, because the only two men who knew what happened, Wallace and himself, would be dead."

Thurston listened without saying a word. When Tye was finished, the major leaned back in his chair and looked into Adam's eyes for several seconds. He stood up, walked to the window and clasped his hands behind his back, staring out at the parade ground. He stood there for a full minute without moving or saying a word. Finally he turned and walked back and sat down in his chair. The chair creaked as he leaned back. He took a cigar out of his breast pocket and lit it. Tilting his head back, he blew a couple rings of smoke that slowly rose to the ceiling.

"This is the way I see it Mr. Carter. You made a big mistake by allowing yourself to be sucked into a plan to rob your boss…but you are young and I think you now know what a mistake it was." Adam nodded and started to say something but Thurston waved his hand with the cigar in it at him. "Let me finish before you say anything. What you did, ended up costing two innocent people their lives whether you had a hand in the actual

190

killing or not. That is a fact, Mr. Carter. More men died at the crossing. I know they deserved what happened, but the fact remains, your decision to rob the Rocking B cost several people their lives. Your actions after the crossing fight tell me you are not a criminal. You are a young man that made a big mistake, and are paying for it everyday." He leaned forward in his chair. "Tye, you say that Wallace has changed his mind and will speak for him?"

"Yes Sir. He will."

"I have a lot of thinking to do Mr. Carter. I do believe you when you say you're truly sorry for what happened, but that doesn't change the fact what resulted from the events at the Rocking B. Now, until I can meet with Mr. Ross, and find out what he is thinking, I am going to have to hold you in the guardhouse."

Adam nodded and quickly unbuckled his gun belt and handed it to the major and sat back down. Thurston went out of his office for minute.

"The major might just give you the biggest break you will ever see in this lifetime, Adam," Tye said. "I don't know what he is going to do, but I know he is a fair man."

Adam nodded his understanding. "I can tell that. He has a lot of pressure trying to keep things going here at the fort. I'm sorry I added to them."

"I was hoping the major would make a decision today one way or another," he thought. *" I don't want to sit in a cell waiting to see when my life will end...or begin anew."* Thurston walked back in and a soldier was with him.

"Private Jackson will escort you to the guardhouse." He wrote a note and gave it to Jackson. "Give this the Corporal Lincoln at the guard house." Adam left with the soldier escorting him.

"Now," Thurston said, "maybe we can see what we can do about finding the man who nearly killed Todd."

"I got a vague description of the man and his horse from him," Tye replied. "I'm going to the saloons in Brackettville and see if anyone might have an idea who it was."

"And then?"

"I'm going after him and bring him back here."

"Dead...or alive?"

"That's up to him. If he gives me any trouble he may be dead. Either way, he's going to be in for a lot of pain."

Thurston smiled. He knew Tye would not kill the man in cold blood, but there was that side of his chief of scouts he had seen before. When he was mad, a lot of bad things could happen. But then, the bastard that did that to the boy deserved whatever Tye would give him. He stood up and shook Tye's' hand. "Good luck. Keep me informed." He then added, "I could send a couple of men with you."

"I had rather go this one by myself, Sir."

Chapter Fourteen

Tye figured the best place to learn information about anyone passing through was the saloons. His good friend owned the largest, so he would start there. Walking across the bridge over Los Moras Creek and into Brackettville, he saw his friend sweeping the wooden walk in front of his saloon.

"Morning, Jim," he hollered.

Jim looked up from sweeping the dust and saw Tye coming toward him. He stopped sweeping and extended his hand. "Top of the morning to you, Tye. Good to see you again."

"I haven't been around a lot here lately."

"So I heard," Jim said. Tye smiled. It never ceased to amaze him that nothing went on in the town or across the road at Fort Clark that Jim didn't know about. "How's the boy doing that had been beat up? I heard he was your nephew."

"He regained consciousness this morning. That's the reason I wanted to talk to you."

"Let's go inside and we'll talk." Only two tables were occupied and they were locals, Tye recognizing their faces except for one youngster. Tye and Jim sat down at a table close to the bar, but far enough away from the other customers that they could talk without being overheard.

"What's on you mind?" Jim asked.

"Like I said a minute ago, Todd came around and we were able to talk to him. He was able to give me a description of the man, but it was vague."

"What did he tell you?"

"That he was a big man and had a full black beard. He wore a hat with the brim pinned up in front, and wore a heavy coat that looked like a buffalo robe. He rode a good looking black horse with a white blaze on his forehead and face."

"That could match a lot of hunters and trappers that come through here." Jim leaned back in his chair trying to remember who might have been here the day of the beating that fit that description. "I wonder," he mumbled. He hollered across the room. "Hey Billy, what kind of horse does that old ex-buffalo hunter Zach whatever his last name is, ride."

"Who?"

"You know, Zach, the big bearded man that smells worse than a damn horse and always wears that buffalo robe no matter if it's hot or cold."

"Zach Robertson?"

"Yeah, that's him. What kind of horse does he ride?

"A black gelding I think."

Jim looked at Tye and Tye asked. "What do you know about him?"

"Not much I'm afraid. He comes in once or twice a week. I know he's a man with a foul temper that goes along with his smell. I've never had a problem with him but I know the owner of the other saloon has."

"Excuse me for a second," Tye said. He stood up and walked over to the man named Billy. He sat down at the table with the man. "What do you know about this Zach fellow?"

"Who the hell are you to be asking?" Billy blurted out. The man sitting next to him spoke up.

"The man is Tye Watkins and I suggest you don't piss him off, so answer his damn question."

"I don't like talking about my friends."

Tye reached across the table and grabbed the young man by the collar, jerked him across the table, to where the man's face was only inches from his. "I'm looking for a man that beat a kid so bad he almost died. He stole the horse that the kid was riding so that makes him a horse thief as well. Now listen to me you piece of horse shit, I will only ask you one more time." The cold edge of Tye's Bowie had appeared from nowhere and touched the man's cheek. Sweat was on Billy's forehead and his eyes were wide with fear. "What can you tell me about this Zach Robertson?" He threw the man back in his chair.

The man named Billy swallowed and rubbed his neck with his hand. "We hunted buffalo a couple years back up north of here. We went our separate ways a year ago, and then one day he shows up here. I only see him when he comes in here."

"Think hard...was he in here three days ago?"

Billy thought for a few seconds. "Yes, I think he was as a mater of fact. Said he was going to Mexico to see someone he knew."

"Does his horse have a white blaze across its face?"

"Yes sir. It looks like a bolt of lightning." Tye looked at Jim and nodded. He walked back to the table where Jim sat.

"Sounds like our man. I'm going to get some supplies and see if I can find him. He turned back to Billy. "Where in Mexico was he going?"

"I'm not sure, but he said it was close to the border and was a small village that this man he knows visits a lot."

"What's this friend's name?"

I just know a last name. Alvarez I think. He is a well known bandit over there."

"Damn," Tye muttered.

"You know him?" Jim asked.

"I don't know him personally, but yeah I know him. He's as bad as they come. His name is Horatio Alvarez. Over here he is known as *The Ghost*, because he and his gang of cutthroats would hit some homesteads over here occasionally and also people traveling the Old Mail Road, and then disappear. When I was with the Rangers, we chased him all up and down the Border. We never caught sight of him. We gave him that nickname because he always seemed to just disappear. He hasn't been over here that I know of in a long time. I figured the Federales had caught up with him or maybe one of his own men killed him."

Jim nodded. "I remember him now. He was a bad one. Back when the Civil War was going on back east and all the soldiers were pulled from Clark, his gang raided around here quite a bit. I saw him once when he came in here with some of his men. He got into a fight and knifed one of my customers."

"I didn't know you had this place then?" Tye said.

"I opened in '60, right before the war broke out. I did right well until the troops were pulled out." He chuckled and added. "I damn near starved to death after that until the war was over and troops from the Ninth Calvary and Forty-First Infantry returned to the Fort."

"Do you remember what Alvarez looked like?"

"Vaguely," Jim answered. "It was a long time ago and I figure he's changed some. He was big, not muscular big, but a big belly. I remember one thing about him he could not change though. He had a scar here," Jim put his finger on his cheek just below his right eye, "And it ran all the way to here," he moved his finger down his cheek to below his jaw bone. "It was a nasty scar, probably made by a knife."

"That will give me something to look for. I know the village Billy said he supposedly hangs out in, at least the one he did a long time ago. Maybe he's still there." Tye turned to leave. "I'm going to tell Thurston about him and pick up some supplies."

Jim stood up and shook Tye's hand. "I hope you find Zach," he said, then added. "You be careful."

"Thanks Jim. I'll see you when I get back."

Tye walked straight to Post Headquarters to see Thurston and tell him about Zach and Alvarez. As he passed the parade grounds he saw Senior Master Sergeant O'Malley putting some recruits through their paces. As usual, the Sergeant was loud and intimidating. O'Malley spotted Tye and called a halt to the training and gave the men an appreciated ten minute break. Tye saw him coming and waited,

"Rebecca told me you were going to town to see if you could find out anything. Did you?"

"Zach Robertson is his name. He's headed to Mexico to meet up with an outlaw named Horatio Alvarez."

"Who is that?"

"Maybe you know him as The Ghost."

"Damn… that Alvarez?" O'Malley pushed the crown of his has up with his finger and whistled. "That's a bad hombre, Tye. He's worse than Alex Vasquez you brought in."

Tye nodded. "So I've heard. I'm on my way now to tell Thurston and get some supplies."

"You're going by yourself?" Tye nodded. "I don't think that's a good idea, Tye. This guy is dangerous and you have more than just yourself to think about now."

"I'm not going after Alvarez. I'm going to find the man who damn near killed my nephew. I had rather be by myself on things like this. I can concentrate on the job at hand and not have to worry about someone else's safety. Besides, if something ever happened to me, I know you would take care of my family and that's a load off any man's mind. I'll see you before I leave, but I want to see Thurston now," he said turning and walking away from the sergeant.

O'Malley shook his head and mumbled. "That man is the most hard- headed and stubborn man I have ever met." He turned to the men and yelled. "Breaks over!. Get your sorry miserable butts over here on the double." Tye looked back and smiled. He knew the sergeant was upset and would probably take it out on the recruits.

After visiting with Thurston, explaining everything including why he was going by himself, he had the paper made out to the quartermaster from Thurston to receive whatever supplies he needed, including a packhorse with a shovel, pick, and other supplies a man would need to pass as a prospector. He needed a reason to be there if the Federales confronted him, and there was a lot of prospecting going on in the mountains.

He walked into the hospital and directly to Todd's bed where Rebecca, Buff, and Mrs. O'Malley were fussing over him. "I found out who did this to you Todd. I'm leaving in a few minutes to see if I can find him." He did not say anything about the possibility of having to face the outlaw, Alvarez. He saw no need to unnecessarily worry Rebecca.

Rebecca hugged him and kissed him on the cheek. She knew there was no need to try and talk him out of going. The truth was, for the first time since she had met Tye, she wanted him to go…wanted him to find the monster that did this to Todd and make him pay for what he had done.

After a few minutes of talking, he said he had to get started. He got Buff's attention and motioned with his head to follow him outside. He hugged Rebecca again and kissed Mrs. O'Malley on the cheek and left with Buff following.

"You take care of Rebecca, Buff. If anything happens, I want to know she and the baby will be okay." Buff was shocked at

Tye's somber look and the words. It was not like Tye to say anything more than watch over her.

"You know I will Tye. What's going on? Is there more to this than you are saying?"

"The man I am after is meeting with a notorious bandit named Alvarez. He's the leader of a band of cutthroats that is as bad as the Vazquez gang was. I just didn't want to worry Rebecca. It just helps me to know that she and the baby will be taken care of."

"You don't worry about that. You just stay alive and come back." He took Tye's hand that had been extended to him. Holding the handshake, he asked. "Do you think it's wise to go by yourself?"

"To be honest with you, probably not, but as you know from being on scout so many times it's easier to do things if you don't have to worry about the safety of others. Worrying about someone else can get you killed."

"I understand, Tye. Just be careful and get back here." Tye nodded and left, headed to the stables. Leaving the stables on Sandy, he headed to the quartermasters. It was almost noon by the time he was ready to leave and he intended to cover a lot of miles by dark.

Tye found a place to camp just before full dark. A thick stand of mesquite was the perfect place. He managed to get Sandy into the middle of the stand without getting him scratched by the sharp needles. The mesquite would keep prying eyes from finding him and the thick stand would prevent anyone from entering without making some noise. He wasn't expecting any trouble, but he hadn't survived all these years by being careless.

After stripping his saddle from Sandy's back he took a brush out of his saddle bag and began brushing the big horse. He started at Sandy's neck and worked his way past his ribs to his flank. He repeated the process on the other side. Loose hair and dust filled the still air around him as he repeatedly brushed an area till all the loose hair was removed. Sandy loved to be brushed and stood perfectly still until his master was finished. Tye stepped back and looked at his horse. He was a magnificent animal standing more than seventeen hands high. He was a sorrel, a reddish brown color with a blonde mane and tail. He was extremely smart and Tye would tell you he understood every word he said. Sandy's alerting Tye to trouble had saved the scouts hide more than once. Ben, Tye's pa, had always said a man can learn a lot by watching the actions of his horse: a nervous twitch of their ears, a snicker or whinny could alert a man if he was watchful for such small things.

Walking over to where his saddle was, he sat down. He took a drink of water from his canteen, chewed on some jerky and thought about things. The village that Billy mentioned where Alvarez stayed was some twenty miles into Mexico. Twenty miles of nothing but trouble: Apache bands, bandits, and worst of all, the Federales could be showing up at any time along the trail. He had no friends over there, no one to turn to if he needed help. He lay down on his blanket and looked up through the branches of the mesquite at the black sky with the stars just beginning to show themselves. He loved lying and looking at the Texas sky when there was no moon like tonight.

"A man could spend a lifetime counting the stars and never finish," he thought. *"They never change in appearance, just move around a little bit. They look the same to me tonight as they did to men a hundred years ago…maybe a thousand."*

He thought of all the nights he had camped alone under those stars picking out constellations that his pa had taught him years ago. There was never a night under the stars that he didn't think of his pa and how much he missed him. Tye was tough, what the Mexicans would call *mucho hombre,* but when he thought of his parents, he always got a lump in his throat and his eyes misted over. This side of Tye, the loving and sentimental side, always amazed Rebecca and his close friends, because each of them knew just how tough and vicious he could be when confronted by someone wanting to harm him or someone he cared for. This side of him is why Rebecca could go anywhere she wanted to go on the fort without the whistles and remarks coming from all sides from the soldiers. They did not want to be the center of Tye's wrath.

A thought suddenly hit Tye.

"Pablo's village is almost in a direct path between the border and the village he is heading to." Tye met Pablo a couple months earlier when he was chasing the outlaw called The Breed. After talking with Pablo he found out that the Mexican's father and his father had been good friends. In fact, Tye being a young boy at the time, remembered the man because of his horse, a solid black gelding whose saddle and bridle was adorned with silver coins. He remembered him as a very nice man and his pa liked him a lot.

"I need to stop by the village and visit with Pablo. Zach may have stopped and he might just be able to give me some recent information on the man." He decided he would go there as soon as he crossed the Rio Grande River.

The night passed quietly and Tye slept well-at least as well as a man can sleep lying on the ground. It was about an hour before the sun would appear when he saddled Sandy. The late fall morning air was crisp and Sandy was being a little frisky indicating to Tye he was ready and wanting to get on the trail. That's what Tye loved about this horse. He had owned other mounts that had rather stay in the stables or if on the trail, stay picketed and eat grass, but not Sandy. This horse was always ready to go.

Second Chance

Tye figured he was two hours from the river and the border and another half hour or so to Pablo's village. The terrain here was tough on a horse and would only get tougher as he closed in on the border. Arroyos, cactus, sage, cliffs, and loose rocks on the sides of the hills made it tough on both horse and rider. In a few places where the footing was the worse, Tye dismounted and led Sandy rather than risk a hoof slipping and both taking a nasty fall.

Midmorning found Tye sitting on Sandy on the crest of a hill overlooking the Rio Grande. This was the exact spot he had chased the outlaw Breed and crossed into Mexico. Giving Sandy a gentle nudge, horse and rider started down the slope to the river. The river this time of the year was less than two feet deep with good footing because of the hard rocky bottom.

Just before reaching the west bank and Mexico, Tye let Sandy drink his fill. Reaching the bank, he dismounted and filled both of his canteens to the brim. He could get some more at the village. He looked at the sun and figured he would be in the village about eleven o'clock. He nudged Sandy into a trot. He looked over his shoulder at Texas disappearing behind the mesquites.

"*I hope that is not my last look at Texas,*" he thought. Rider and horse now entered the forbidden land where there were many enemies of any white man traveling here-and few friends.

Chapter Fifteen

'PABLO! PABLO!" shouted a young man who was working in a garden just on the outskirts of the small village. "YOU'RE FRIEND RETURNS TO OUR VILLAGE." Villagers stopped what they were doing and waved to Tye as he entered the village. He was sort of a hero to them because the outlaw Breed that he captured and took back to be hung, was hated in the village. The Breed had killed a very popular resident of the village a year or so earlier that left a wife with no husband, and two children with no father. If Tye had not taken him back to Texas, he would have been a victim of the angry villagers and their razor sharp machetes. When word reached the village that Breed was dead, a great celebration was held.

Pablo came out of his adobe home and waved at Tye. Tye could see only the white of Pablo's teeth because of the huge grin that spread across the man's face. Tye dismounted and met his friend with a handshake followed by big hug from Pablo. Tye pushed the much smaller man back and put his hands on each of the little man's shoulders.

"How is my friend?" Tye asked.

"Good…and you?'

Tye nodded. "It's good to see you again my friend."

"I am glad to see you…the whole village is glad to see you," he said waving his hand at the residents who had gathered behind them.

"Come into my home," Pablo said. He then turned to a young boy, "Juan, take our friends horse and take care of him." Tye had to duck to keep from banging his head on the door facing as he entered. "Consuelo, bring some frijoles and bread." They sat down at the table. "It is good to see you Tye, but I am afraid to ask why you are here so far from your home."

"My fourteen year old nephew was beaten almost to death and his horse stolen by the man I am after."

Pablo was shocked. "What sort of man would do this?"

"A sorry excuse for one I would say," Tye replied.

"What does this man have to do with my village?" Pablo asked.

"A friend of his said he told him he was going to see an old friend, Horatio Alvarez who stayed in a village west of here."

Pablo looked shocked. The bandito, Alvarez?" Tye nodded. "Sweet Mother of Mary," he mumbled. "This is a very bad hombre, Tye. He has killed many innocent villagers all over Mexico."

"I know that and he killed many people in my State a few years ago. I chased him before when I was with the Rangers."

"You are going after him by yourself?"

"I'm by myself, but no, I am not after him. I am only after a man named Zach Robertson. I will avoid any confrontation with the outlaw if possible."

Consuelo brought the frijoles, bread, and water to the table with a big smile for Tye.

"Gracious, Consuelo," the scout said. "Have any strangers passed through here the last couple days or so?" he asked, looking back at Pablo.

"None that I know of, but I will ask around. You rest for a few minutes and eat. I will be back shortly." Many of the people of his village were still in the street, curious as to why the scout from Fort Clark was back. Pablo addressed the villagers. "Our friend seeks a man who almost killed his nephew and stole the boy's horse. Have any of you seen a stranger, a white man, the last three days?"

A very short, elderly man stepped forward. "Si, Pablo. Two days ago a white man passed near my home. I watched him from the hill where my goats were."

Pablo walked to the old man. "Come into my house Joaquin, and meet with my friend and tell him what you saw." He put his arm around the older man as they walked to his home.

Entering his home he walked to the table where Tye was sitting. "Tye, this is my friend Joaquin who lives near here." He turned to Joaquin and speaking in Spanish, asked him to tell Tye what he saw.

The little man answered, looking at Tye and speaking in Spanish which Pablo interpreted. Tye could understand some but not all as the man spoke.

"He says," Pablo interpreted, "that two days ago while watching his goat herd, a white man passed near his home which is just about a half mile from here."

"Ask him what the man looked like and also the horse he was riding," Tye asked.

Pablo repeated what Tye said and the man spoke again. When he was through, Pablo spoke.

"He says he looked like a very big man and wore a heavy coat which he thought was strange because it was warm. He had a black beard and was not close enough to see any thing else. He rode a black horse and led another horse which he does not remember the color. Tye stood up and walked around the table and shook the man's hand.

"Gracious my friend," he said. The little man nodded and walked out the door. "He pretty well described the man I'm after."

"The village you look for where Alvarez stays is a day's ride west of here." Tye nodded and sat back down and finished his frijoles.

"I think I have been there before, but it was a long time ago. I was with my father then."

"Will you stay with us for awhile?"

"I'd like to, but I need to find this man as soon as possible. I'll be leaving in a few minutes. I want to thank you again for your and Consuelo's hospitality. I really appreciate it."

"Do not hesitate to call on me or anyone in this village anytime. We owe you for bringing the Breed to justice. We think of you as one of us."

Tye knew that a great compliment for a Mexican to consider a white man one of them. "That is appreciated, Pablo. Like I told you the last time I was here, if you or your village need me, just send a messenger to Fort Clark. I told the Post Commander about you and your village. He will let me know if you need me." A young boy appeared at the door and spoke in pretty good English.

"Senor Tye. Your horse is outside and ready."

Tye stood up and handed the boy a gold coin. "Gracious." He walked outside and mounting Sandy leaned down and shook Pablo's hand. "You and your friends are friends of mine. I owe you." He rode out of the village with the people waving at him. Once out of the village he reined Sandy to a halt and looking back, waved, and then headed Sandy west, deeper into Mexico, deeper into the forbidden land.

Second Chance

When the sun was a little past its zenith, he came to a small creek. He dismounted, letting Sandy drink from the clear water. Tye knelt and cupped his and got a handful of the water. He was surprised how cool it was. As he swallowed a couple handfuls he figured it was runoff from the snow in the higher mountains and probably was dry most of the year. He knew the weather had been crazy this year. He had heard the mountains here in Mexico and up around Fort Davis which was two hundred miles northwest of Fort Clark, had received some early snow but then warm weather had set in. That was probably why this creek had the water in it.

He looked at the hills he was in now and to the west where the mountains were shrouded in a blue haze. He was twenty to thirty miles from the base of them. He would be there by this time tomorrow. He stepped back in the saddle and made a clicking noised with his mouth and Sandy crossed the small, shallow creek.

~~

Forty miles due west, in the small village of Los Cantos, Zach Robertson sat in the cantina with his friend Alvarez. The cantina was empty except for two other men, both who were members of Alvarez's gang. Drinking tequila, the two men had been reminiscing about the past and reliving old stories of when they last rode together. After laughing about one story, Alvarez's mood changed a little.

"You have not told me why you come here to see me after all this time has passed."

Zach downed the last drop of tequila in his glass and wiped his mouth with the filthy sleeve of his coat. "Just got bored in Texas. With the Comanche raiding up north on the plains, it got plum dangerous to hunt buffalo unless you were with a large party of hunters. I did okay trapping for awhile along the border but that got to be too much work. I never was one to like work if you remember." Alvarez nodded and smiled.

Zach chuckled some over the remark, but it was true. He had never done an honest days work in his life. He always thought work was for someone else to do and he would just sit back and take whatever they made. I decided, if you wanted me, I would ride with you. You and me are alike, to damn lazy to work."

The fat senorita that ran the cantina came over and refilled their glasses and put some more sliced lemons on the plate with salt.

"I can use a man like you Zach, but it's been a long time since I saw you. I don't go into Texas anymore."

"I know that and I wondered why?"

"I could say it was because of the army but that would not be entirely true. The Federales over here are stupid and a lot of the so called leaders, the high ranking officers, are bigger crooks than we are so it makes it easier to operate over here. But to be honest, the real reason is the big scout at Fort Clark, Tye Watkins. He caught several of my men when we were raiding over there. He's relentless once he gets on a trail and he's a better tracker than most Apaches are. I put a bounty on him once and no one could collect it. Several tried, several good men, but they failed. I am not afraid of him but I see no sense in asking for trouble by raiding over there when we do alright here."

Zach nodded. "I know this Watkins feller. Not personally, but his good friend owns a saloon there in Brackettville that I visited frequently. He and all the people that frequent the place are always talking about the man like he was all powerful, almost God like. I saw him a couple times and he looked like any other man, just a little bigger than most."

Alvarez smiled. "He's not normal Zach. I can promise you that. I had some good men that he killed or captured. He is not the normal army scout. I've been intending to ask you about that horse you were leading when you came here and I kept forgetting about it. Where did you get it?"

Zach laughed. "I took it from a boy about fifteen years old or so that I met on the Old Mail Road."

Alvarez asked. "This here youngster just let you take him?"

214

"Well…he did put up a little fight." He pointed to the bruise on his cheek. "The little shit could hit pretty hard. After he hit me I beat the hell out of him and left him off the road behind some sage and cactus."

"Was he dead?"

"I don't think so, unless he died later."

Alvarez stood up. "I would like for you to stay but I'm afraid I am going to have to ask you to leave."

"LEAVE!" Zach screamed and stood up quickly. The other two other men jumped up and stood with their hands on their guns. "Why in hell should I leave?"

"The damn brand on that horse was U.S. Army. I guarantee that kid you beat up and maybe killed lived on the fort and was probably an officer's brat. If that's the case, Watkins may be on your trail now."

"He wouldn't come into Mexico."

Alvarez leaned forward and put his hands on the table. He was running out of patience and he was not used to not being obeyed immediately and with no arguments.
He asked Zach. "You ever hear of the outlaws Alex Vasquez or The Breed?"

"I've heard of them."

"Watkins tracked them into Mexico and captured both of them and they ended up hanging." Zach did not know that, and didn't know what to say. "I don't need trouble with the United States Army or the Watkins fellow either," Alvarez added.

"I...I don't have anywhere to go," a suddenly subdued Zach replied.

"I have a cabin about five miles from here. I will get you some supplies and have one of my men show you where it is. I'll give you supplies for a week. If you have not heard from me by then come back down here. I figure if Watkins is on your tail, he will be here today or tomorrow, or the next day at the latest. He turned to the men in the room. "Juan, get some supplies for a week for one man and show Zach where the cabin is and then come on back." He turned back to Zach. "If everything is okay, I will see you in a few days." He turned back to the one man still there. His name was Lupe and was one of Alvarez's best, most dependable men. "Lupe, come over here I need you to do something for me." Lupe walked over to the table. "Sit," Alvarez said. "Consuelo, please bring another round of tequila. When the drinks came and each had a shot, Alvarez leaned forward and spoke quietly so Consuelo could not hear. "I want you to take two men and go back down the trail a few miles. If a white man shows up on the trail, kill him and bring him to me."

"Who is this man you want killed?"

"It might be the scout from Fort Clark, Tye Watkins." Lupe sat his glass of tequila down on the table hard, spilling some of it.

"He is bad medicine…a dangerous man to tangle with."

"I know that, and that's why I am sending my best man to take care of him…with some help also."

"You don't want him alive?"

"Hell no. I don't want to chance getting you or anyone else killed. Shoot the sonofabitch from ambush and be done with it and don't take any chances."

Lupe stood up. "I'll take care of it." He left to make arrangements for supplies for a couple days and get two men he could depend on.

~~

Back at Fort Clark, things were returning to normal. Todd, after some good meals was doing fine. The doctor would probably release him from the hospital tomorrow. Rebecca, with the exception of some back pains, was doing fine. The doctor, who examined her this morning, said she would have the baby in a week to ten days.

Major Thurston had met with Bill Ross about Adam Carter. Wallace had already had long talks with Bill and Lester about the

Carter situation. The old man was upset as hell at first but the more he listened to what his long time friend said, the more he calmed down. After listening to Major Thurston's thoughts on the situation he reluctantly agreed to what Thurston wanted to do. Bill understood that the men who killed his wife and son were dead. He also understood young people could make wrong decisions sometimes. He knew that at a point in his life, he could have taken up the outlaw trail himself. He, Wallace, and Lester were heading back to the Rocking B today. They had been gone way to long. On the way out of the fort, Wallace stopped at the guardhouse to see Adam. He was glad Ross had agreed with Thurston about Adam having to join the army, but Ross told him not to tell Adam. He thought it would do the young man some good to worry a little longer about what was going to happen to him.

"Mr. Ross understands people sometimes make mistakes, especially young people," Wallace said to Adam as the two shook hands through the bars of the cell. "He's not going to forget that your mistake cost him his family, so he doesn't want to see you again. I guess that means I won't be seeing you either. I just wanted to thank you one more time for saving my butt from those Comanche the other day"

Adam nodded his head. "We're even, Wallace. I'd be dead if you and Tye had not gotten me off of that hill." The two men shook hands and without another word, Wallace left. Adam stood there, watching through the bars as Wallace walked away. He was disappointed that Wallace didn't know, or didn't say if he knew what decision Thurston and Ross had reached. He had been sure the rancher would not forgive him and he would hang, but maybe, with what Wallace said, there was hope for him. He could not blame him one bit if he hadn't agreed. My stupidity cost him his family.

He sat down on the wooden bed and stared at the floor. He had never been a religious man. Oh, he believed in God and all that, but as far as going to Church and praying all the time and telling others about his beliefs…no.   At this moment in his life though, he looked up at the ceiling saying, "Lord, if it is in your plan and things work out for me, I promise you from this day forward, Your name will not be far from my heart. He realized that he felt different, lighter on his feet. He felt things were going to be okay. He lay down on his bunk and quickly drifted off to sleep.

~~

The trail Tye was following was plain enough. Lots of people and even a few wagons used it to get to and from the village. He was giving Sandy his head and let him follow the road. Tye was more interested in what was in the bushes and on the sides of the hills. He was over half way to his destination when he figured he had better start looking for a place to throw his bedroll. There would be no camp fire tonight. He didn't want to have a traveler accidentally come into his camp, so he was looking away from the trail for a suitable place.

The sun was only half visible over the mountains when he decided he wasn't going to find the perfect place. He reined Sandy to the left, off the trail. He wanted to be at least a hundred yards from the trail so any horse coming down the trail would not smell Sandy and vice versa. Horses had a tendency to snort, stomp their hooves and make all kinds of noise when they smelled or heard a strange horse.

Just to be on the safe side, Tye took Sandy over a hundred yards into the brush. He stripped the saddle, brushed him for a few minutes and then gave him some water from his hat. There was enough grass for him to munch to keep him occupied for awhile. Tye spread his bedroll and placed his saddle where he could use it for a pillow. There was just enough light left for him to clean his Colt and Henry, make sure they worked properly and were loaded. Cleaning his weapons almost every night was something that carried over from his pa. "You may have the best gun made, but if it jams because of filth, it ain't worth a damn and liable to get you killed," he heard his pa say countless times. Tye took that lesson to heart and practiced it religiously.

He lay there chewing his jerky, thinking about tomorrow. *"I cannot just go riding into the village, so I will find a place to watch…to observe what is going on and see if any white men are there. If Zach is there, I'm sure he as no idea me or anyone else is looking for him. He's probably feeling as safe as a bear cub with its mother right now. I hate to bust your bubble Zach, but fire and brimstone is fixing to rein down on you if you are there."* Tye was still madder than hell about what the bastard done to Todd but he had control of his emotions-right now anyway. He shut his eyes, trusting Sandy to alert him of anyone or anything coming close to camp.

~~

Less than a mile behind Tye, a Mexican followed riding a donkey. In a worn out old scabbard on his back was a twenty-four inch machete. In his hand he carried an old single shot Sharps that had belonged to his father. He wore the usual white clothes of a farmer with a straw sombrero on his head. Pablo was following his friend, Tye, suspecting the man might run into more trouble than he could handle. As soon as Tye left his small village he had gathered a few supplies, kissed Consuelo goodbye, threw a blanket on his donkey, and followed him. He was sure Tye would be unhappy at his following, so he decided he would stay just far enough away to watch his friends back in case of trouble.

He traveled until dark and made camp just off the well traveled road. He was a farmer and a herder of goats and it never entered his mind to camp a good ways from the road so he would not be seen. He only wanted to be close by if his friend got into trouble. He spread his blanket on the ground and lay down, but even as tired as he was, sleep would not come. Lying there, looking at the black sky with its million stars, doubt entered his mind. *"He wondered why he had thought he could help his friend: he had never hit another man in anger and certainly never shot anyone. How could he help Tye? He was a simple farmer, not a warrior. What would happen to Consuelo and his children if he was killed?"* That thought made him sit up. *"Maybe I should go back home. Tye is a fighting man and has taken care of himself for years. He doesn't need me, a farmer who knows nothing about such things, to watch his back. I would probably only be a worry to him if he knew I was here."* With these thoughts, he started to get up, hesitated, and lay back down. *"Tye did not know me when he risked his life to prevent the outlaw named Breed from killing me. We are friends now and is helping not what friends do?"* He lay back down, determined that he would stay and help... if he could.

Chapter Sixteen

The sky was filled with stars as Tye looked up through the branches and leaves. The moon was only a sliver of light. It was the time of the month of a new moon. He had woke up and lay very still; trying to figure out what had awaken him. Sandy was quiet so no one was close to camp. He raised himself up and looked around. Seeing nothing, he sat perfectly still, listening for any unusual sounds. He heard no sound other than the light night time breeze rustling the leaves, and an occasional small varmint scurrying around.

Something had awakened him and he was a little uptight about what it had been. He reached over and slipped his Colt out of the holster, pulled on his Apache moccasin boots and stood up. Walking over to Sandy, he put his hand on the horse's neck. Sandy nuzzled Tye's shoulder as the scout stood there looking, listening.

After five minutes he decided there had been nothing unusual and he woke up for no reason. He placed his Colt back in the holster and leaving his boots on, lay back down pulling the wool blanket up to his chin. The night air had a chill to it and the blanket felt good.

After twenty minutes of laying there awake, he knew he was not going back to sleep. He looked at the stars that were beginning to fade this time of the morning and figured it to be about four o'clock. He saddled Sandy, gathered his belongings and placed them in the saddle bags. He checked his Henry and Colt and stepped into the saddle. He was leaving earlier than he figured so he would probably be at the village by noon.

About fifteen minutes of working his way around mesquites and sage from where he camped, he was back on the trail. It was still plenty dark with the sun still two hours away. He had put on his leather jacket to ward off the chill and dampness of the morning. It was quiet, real quiet. The only sound was Sandy's hooves striking a rock here and there and the squeaking of the saddle. Tye, unlike the soldiers, carried no items on him that rattled or reflected sunlight. He had no crossed sword emblem on his hat like the soldiers did. The only thing on him that was metal was his bullets in the belt, the Colt in his holster, and his trusty Bowie sheathed inside his right boot. The handle on it was wood, not metal. He even had the buckles on his bridle and saddle painted black. He survived all these years by doing little things like that. Very few things in nature reflected sunlight and not being seen was mostly a good thing.

Several hours later, when the sun was almost overhead, he saw it. Most men would have kept on riding, not paying much attention to his surroundings. He was always alert, always watchful. This had been one of the many lessons his pa had taught him. At any time when they were traveling together, he might tell Tye to shut his eyes and describe what was around him. That was the way it was with men in his profession. That is how they stayed alive.

Before him, the trail entered a canyon, not unlike many he had passed through up to now, but something about this one made Tye leery. He could not put his finger on it, but something told him there was danger ahead and he always trusted his gut feelings. He sat on Sandy and searched both sides and rims of the canyon. He watched Sandy closely for any signs he might see or hear anything. Nothing seemed to be wrong, but he continued sitting in the saddle, looking. He couldn't shake the feeling danger was near. He reached in the saddle bags, taking out the binoculars.

Hidden from view, Lupe watched the gringo from about a hundred yards away. He had his rifle already cocked and the barrel sticking through thick branches of the sage bush. The scout's head was in the "V" of his rifles sights. He wanted a little closer shot, so he waited. He could not figure out what had caused the man to stop and just sit there on his horse. Had the gringo seen something? He turned his head slowly and looked across the canyon to where his two men were hidden. They were to shoot only after he did and only if he missed. Looking where they were hidden, he could see no way the gringo had spotted them.

As he watched, he uttered an oath under his breath. He saw the gringo take the binoculars out and began to search the walls of the canyon. Without knowing for sure, he knew this man to be the scout, Watkins, and he was not going to take a chance on giving him a break. Lupe was an excellent shot with a rifle and was confident he could drop the man from here. He exhaled slowly and relaxed, holding his breath. He slowly squeezed the trigger. The rifle bucked against his shoulder and the bullet sliced though the air toward its target.

Pablo sat on his donkey watching Tye from a stand of mesquite. He also was trying to figure out why his friend had stopped and just sat there. Lupe had left even earlier than Tye had this morning. He could not sleep either. He thought the main reason was it had been a long time since he slept anywhere except in his bed with his wife. Lying on the ground was a little different from lying on a soft mattress.

As he watched Tye, from the corner of his eye he saw a puff of smoke high on the cliff to his right and a second later, the report of a rifle. He watched his friend tumble from his magnificent horse and his heart stopped in fear for the scout. He waited a couple seconds to see if his friend moved. Seeing no movement and fearing the worse, he started out of the mesquites to see if he could help when he saw a man coming down the slope. He backed into the mesquite and watched, a lump in his throat- as he looked at the still, prone body of his friend being watched over by his horse. He stood over him as if to protect his master. When Pablo glanced back at the man who was coming toward Tye, he saw two more men coming from the other side of the canyon.

He watched the three men approach cautiously, rifles ready to go into action in a split second if the man moved. The horse shied away from the men when they were a few feet from Tye. He heard the lone man tell the others to keep their guns on the man. He walked to Tye and with the toe of his boot, flipped the scout over on his back.

Pablo and the man saw immediately Tye was not dead. The bullet had creased his skull just above the ear and he was unconscious. Pablo could see his chest move as he breathed. As he watched, the man rolled Tye back on his stomach and grabbed both of Tye's wrists, tying them behind his back. After tying Tye's hands, he motioned for the two other men to come to him. One of the men grabbed Sandy's reins and led the skittish horse to where Tye lay. The two of them lifted Tye up and across the saddle. They untied his hands and tossed the rope under the horse and with a man on each side, tied the scouts hands and feet to each other, securing Tye so he would not fall off. Retrieving their horses, they mounted and leading Sandy with Tye lying across his saddle, headed for the village. Pablo watched them leave and swore that somehow, someway, he would help his friend.

~~

Rebecca, taking a midday nap, suddenly sat up straight in bed screaming, "NO…NO!" Buff, sitting at the table almost jumped out of his skin. Jumping up from his chair, he ran into the bedroom to find Rebecca hysterical.

"What's the matter, Rebecca?" he asked sitting on the bed and hugging her to his chest. "What is it? What's wrong?"

"Tye," she sobbed. "It's Tye'

"What are you talking about?"

"Tye's hurt."

Buff pulled away and with his hands on her shoulders, looking her straight in the eye, asked. "What makes you think he is hurt?"

"A woman knows, Buff," she sobbed. "I was asleep and I felt the hurt…Tye's hurt."
She begins sobbing even more.

"Rebecca, honey. You were dreaming. Tye's fine. Now calm down and relax. You don't need to be this upset." He pulled her to him and she buried her face in his chest, sobbing uncontrollably. He was doing his best to calm her but didn't really know what to say or do. Never being married, the whys and wherefores of what women do did not exactly fit in his realm of expertise.

After two more minutes of sobbing she began to calm down. Buff continued to hold her tight, and massaged her back with his hands. When he thought she was calm enough, he lay her back down on the bed. She rolled into the fetal position and just lay there, breathing hard.

"Buff," she said. "Can you get Mrs. O'Malley?"

"Be right back." He practically ran out of the room and out of the house heading to the O'Malley's. He was back with her in less than ten minutes. He had told her what Rebecca was upset about.

He sat down at the table while Mrs. O'Malley went into the room and shut the door. He could hear them talking but could not make out what they were saying.

" *That was crazy,* " he thought to himself. "*Crazy and scary as hell. I know she sure doesn't need to get that upset with the baby this close. What made her think Tye was hurt all of a sudden. Why did she...* his thought were interrupted by the door to the bedroom being opened.

Mrs. O'Malley had her arm around Rebecca's shoulder helping her walk. "Buff, can you stand on the other side and help me hold her up. We need to get her to the hospital."

"What's the matter?" Buff asked as he moved to the opposite side of Rebecca to help.

"Her stomach is hurting and I thought it best if the doctor looked at her," She said. Nothing else was said as they made their way to the hospital. The doctor was there and they-the doc and Mrs. O'Malley-placed Rebecca in a bed. Buff walked to the waiting area and sat down while the doc examined Rebecca behind the curtains. Fifteen minutes later, Mrs. O'Malley came out saying she was going to Rebecca's house to get some things that she needed.

"The doctor thought it was best she spend the rest of the day and tonight here where she could be watched."

"Is...Is she okay?" a very concerned Buff asked.

Mrs. O'Malley simply nodded. Her not saying anything raised Buff's concern even more, but all he could do now was wait, and pray she was okay.

Chapter Seventeen

Lupe sent one of the men with him ahead to the village to tell Alvarez the good news about the scout. He looked back at the unconscious Tye lying across the saddle and told himself that the scout was not the exalted God-like man he had heard so much about. He's just a man that bleeds like me and every other man. He sure as hell went down like any other man when my bullet creased him. He laughed and hollered at Jesse, the man with him who was bringing up the rear. "What do you think of the great scout now?"

Jesse smiled, his brown, tobacco stained teeth showing through a full black   beard that was in great need of a trim.

"He ain't much I'd say." They were riding into the village when Lupe saw Alvarez standing in the middle of the narrow road that wound through the little village.

When the little caravan approached Alvarez, he walked around Lupe's horse to where Tye was. He grabbed a handful of black hair and raised his head to where he could see his face. He knew it was Watkins from the descriptions he had gotten from a dozen different men. "Good work, Lupe." He looked at Jesse. "Get someone to help you put him that shed over there. You stand guard at the door until I send someone to replace you, and heaven help you if you let him escape." Jesse nodded and left to get another man to help him carry the scout into the shed. Alvarez turned to Lupe. "Step down my friend, you deserve a drink." They walked to the cantina.

Pablo cautiously entered the village, but no one paid him a mind. He looked like any other resident of the village in his white shirt, white pants, sandals, and sombrero. Most everyone's attention was on watching the men carry Tye into a shed and coming back out, locking the door behind them. Jesse sat down by the door and two men who had helped him left for the cantina. Jesse had ridden with Alvarez for the last four years and he knew the man meant what he said he would do if the gringo escaped. He would not let that happen.

Tye slowly began to regain consciousnesses. The first thing he noticed was a painful pounding in his head. He felt of the side of his head with his hand. His hair was stiff with dried blood and he could feel the cut in his temple where the bullet passed just above his ear. He was a little confused and was tried to get his thoughts straight as to what happened, and where he was. He lay still because he found out the hard way that any movement of his head caused immediate pain. Moving only his eyes he tried to figure out where he was. He knew it was a wooden building of some kind because light came between the boards. His wrists were burning some and when he looked, he realized they appeared to be rope burned. He guessed his wrists had been tied when he was brought here-where ever here was.

He shut his eyes and tried to remember what happened. Slowly the pieces begin to fall into place. He was on Sandy looking ahead at was probably the most obvious ambush canyon he had ever seen. If he was hunting Apaches he would not have gone into it for any reason. He wasn't though, he was hunting a white man, and a man who he did not think even knew anyone was following him, so he discounted the thought of an ambush. But, he could not shed the feeling of danger so he took out his binoculars and scanned both sides of the canyon. He was looking high on the right side when he saw it; a flash of sunlight off something and then the smoke. He threw himself to the right but it was too late. He felt the bullet hit, then everything went black. He knew he had been lucky to move the instant the man fired the rifle or he would be lying back on the trail with a hole in his head.

He could hear voices, some of whom were obviously children, all speaking Spanish. He could speak a little of the language and understood enough to get by, but that was all. The children meant he was in a village, but which one. He wondered who had ambushed him. If it was bandits, they would have killed him and left him on the trail for the buzzards and varmints. If it had been Anderson, he would have done the same as the bandits. He was totally confused about what happened, who did it, and where he was. For a man who always was in control of things this was a nightmare. He knew he was going to play out the unconscious thing for as long as he could. If anyone poked their heads in to check on him he was going to pretend to still be out.

He thought of trying to go to sleep, but listening to the talk outside, a man's name caught his attention-Alvarez. He listened trying to pick up the conversation of at least two men outside his door. They mentioned Alvarez again and then his heart skipped a beat when he heard Zach's name mentioned. Zach was in the village and from what he could understand from the men; Alvarez suspected someone might be following Zach. So it was Alvarez that had him ambushed.

"If I get out of this he's going to pay." Tye thought. *" I wasn't that concerned about him, but that sure as hell has changed now that he tried to kill me."*

He raised his head a little and the pain was a lot less than it was earlier. That fact encouraged him and considering his present situation, he needed some. He sat up slowly, a little dizzy at first, but it went away quickly. He sat there a full two minutes before he stood up and very carefully and quietly, made his way to the door. The cracks between the boards were just wide enough for him to see parts of the village. He could see the backs of the two men who were talking, but not their faces. He looked through the other side of the door and could see people milling about and some small children playing in the yard of one of the houses. He moved farther along the wall and looked through another crack and saw a Mexican man leaning against the hitching post in front of what appeared to be a cantina. The man was holding the reins of a donkey. Tye stared at the man because something about him looked familiar. As he watched, the man took off his sombrero and with a kerchief from his pocket, wiped his face.

"What the hell," Tye thought. *"That's Pablo. What's he doing here?"* Then he remembered. *"Pablo asked if I wanted him to go with me. He was very concerned about me going alone with so many bandits."* Tye smiled. *"That old man is a sight for sore eyes and I bet he knows where I am because he has looked no where else except here."* He looked around for something to signal him with but saw nothing he could use in the semi-darkness of the building.

He heard one of the men at the door speak Alvarez's name again and he moved back to the door and looked through the crack again. He saw two men approaching; a tall lanky man and heavy set one.

"That has to be Alvarez," he thought and hurried back to where he was lying before and lay down, trying to remember just what position he was in.

"Open the door," he heard one of the men say who he figured was Alvarez. He shut his eyes as the door opened.

"He hasn't moved since I put him down," Tye heard one of the men say.

"You let me know when this gringo dog wakes up. Is that clear?" the man Tye figured was Alvarez ordered, and he noticed a lot of emphasis was put on the last three words. The door shut and Tye opened his eyes just enough to make sure no one was in the room with him before he opened them all the way and sat up.

"Somehow, someway, I have to make contact with Pablo. I don't want him to do anything foolish like get himself caught or killed." He stood up and made his way back to the wall he had looked through and saw Pablo a few minutes ago. Pablo was not at the hitching post, but his donkey was still there. Tye carefully made his way all the way around the shed and peering out of any cracks he could find, but saw no sign of Pablo. He noticed the sun was dropping behind the hills. *"I must have been out for quite awhile,"* he thought.

He heard a noise at the door and hurried back to where he was lying, barely getting down and in position before the door opened. Three men walked in with a lantern and looked Tye over. "He is still out," one said.

Another spoke. "Throw the rope over the beam in the ceiling. Alvarez wants him tied so there is no chance of him escaping. They grabbed Tye under the armpits and lifted him to his feet, holding him upright while another tied his hands to the rope. With the other end over the ceiling beam they pulled the rope tight and Tye hung there, his feet barely touching the floor. They tied the rope off and left, leaving Tye hanging helpless from the beam.

~~

Rebecca's pain had subsided to the point where she was fairly comfortable in bed in the hospital. Mrs. O'Malley, sitting in a chair, held her hand. Rebecca did not know how she could have handled the pain today and everything else that had gone along with her pregnancy the last few months if her friend had not been around. She had been a great comfort to her and because of her, Rebecca always knew what to expect next.

"Are you feeling better?" Mrs. O'Malley asked. She had dozed off sitting beside the bed holding Rebecca's hand when Rebecca's movement had awaken her.

Rebecca nodded. "Much better."

"What prompted you to think Tye was hurt?

"I was asleep and all of a sudden I had this cold feeling go through me. It was like my blood turned to ice water. I woke up and just knew something happened. It scared me and I guess I just panicked."

Mrs. O'Malley leaned toward her friend and hugged her. "I had that happen to me once during the War when Mr. O'Malley was at the battle of Bull Run. I just knew he had been killed. It was like a knife in my heart. But, as you know, he was fine just like Tye is now. Everything will be fine and your man will be back...you'll see. Now get some more sleep. Sleep is the best medicine for you."

"Why don't you go home? The kids need you."

"I will when Buff gets back. He's going to stay the night with you. I tell you Rebecca, that old man is a godsend to you and Tye and not just because he has a lot of stories about Tye's pa."

"I know that. I told him once that for a man who never married, he sure knows all the proper things to say to make a woman feel better when she's feeling down in the dumps." Both ladies laughed just as the curtain was pulled back and Buff walked in.

"Well, speak of the devil," Mrs. O'Malley said and hugged the old trapper's neck. Buff was wondering what was going on.

"What's this about the devil?"

"Nothing," Mrs. O'Malley said laughing. "I'll see you two in the morning." She started to leave, but turned back and kissed Buff on the cheek. "Thanks for being here Buff."

"You're welcome," Buff said, a little confused about things.

"Give me a hug you old coot," Rebecca said holding her arms out. Buff gave her a little hug but Rebecca pulled him tight to her. "Thanks for being here Buff. It means the world to me."

Buff gave her a little squeeze and stepped back and looked at her. "OLD COOT?"They both laughed. "Looks like you are feeling a little better. You gave me...I mean you gave all of us quite a scare. Todd is worried sick about you."

"I'm much better Buff. Why don't you go tell him I'm fine and then come back."

"I don't have to, he's here. I couldn't make him stay home." He raised his voice a little and said. "Come on in here Todd."

Todd hobbled in through the curtain that gave her some privacy. He looked better, but she could tell he was still hurting. He came over to the bed and they hugged for a full minute, both crying. He pulled back.

"Now, don't you go getting all upset again," he said, tears running down his bruised and swollen face.

She grabbed his arm and pulled him back and gave him another hug and felt at peace for the first time in a while. Tye was away but she now felt he was okay and she had friends here than cared for her and her for them. "What more could I ask?" she asked herself.

Chapter Eighteen

Tye's hands had no feeling in them. He knew if he did not do something pretty quick they could be permanently damaged. It would be too dark in the room before long to see anything. He looked at the ceiling and at the beam he was hanging from. There might just be enough room for him to squeeze between the beam and the ceiling. With great effort, he swung his legs up to the beam. As soon as he was upside down, his head started pounding again. It took all his strength to work the lower part of his body over the beam. It felt as if his skin was being ripped as his upper body worked its way through the tight space between the ceiling and the beam. Finally over the beam, he silently dropped to the dirt floor then sat down and began untying the ropes from his hands with his teeth. Fifteen long minutes later his hands were free, burning as the blood rushed back in. He rubbed them against each other long enough to get the feeling back in them.

While sitting there he heard a thump, followed by another one. Tye jumped up and stood to the side of the door intending to jump whoever came through the door.

A whispered voice came through the door.

"Tye...Tye...it's me, Pablo. Can you hear me?"

It was the sweetest words Tye had heard in a long time. "I hear you," Tye answered softly. He heard the bolt on the door slide and the door opened and Pablo stepped in. Tye hugged the little man. "Let's get out of here," Tye whispered. Tye picked up the rifle from the man Pablo had knocked out as well as his bandoleer. The loops were more than half full of shells. He also took a knife from the sheath on the man's hip. He felt much better now that he was armed, forgetting about his headache. Like ghosts, the two made their way out of the village.

Pablo had taken his donkey shortly after dark to a spot about a half mile from the village. He had some food and water in his pack. Tye was dying of thirst. He had not had a drop to drink since before he was shot and that was hours ago. Taking the gourd that contained the water, he drank greedily, immediately feeling better. He stuck out his hand and pumped Pablo's.

"I don't know why you came, but I'm sure glad you did my friend. You saved my life today. I owe you."

"Si." Pablo said grinning. "I did save your butt today, didn't I.? He reached up and patted the much taller man on the shoulder. "We are even. You saved me from the bandito, Breed, remember?"

Tye smiled and nodded. "I remember." It was dark and he could not see much, but he knew they needed to move farther into the brush. "Let's move a little deeper into this brush." A few minutes later he was satisfied and they picketed the donkey and made a cold camp.

"What is the plan now?" Pablo asked.

"I want you to go back to your village and Consuelo. Things are going to get pretty nasty here and I don't want to worry about you getting mixed up in it and maybe hurt."

Pablo said. "I thought you were just going to find the man that hurt your nephew?"

Tye nodded. "That was before they tried to kill me. Not doing it was a big mistake on their part."

"You are one man and they are many."

"I'm not going to take them on all at once, Pablo. I don't have to be in a hurry. I intend to take them on like the Apache does: one or two at a time and by surprise."

"I understand, I have heard of your reputation as a fighter and that you are as much Apache as the Apache, but what about your back? Do you not need someone to watch it.?"

Tye knew Pablo was right, but he wanted him to be out of harms way. "Have you ever killed a man Pablo?"

"No. I have not," the little man answered, "But I have never hit a man like I did that guard tonight either." Tye started to say something else, but chuckled instead.

He put his hands on the shoulders of the elderly Mexican and smiled as he looked down at him. "You win, but you will have to promise me you will stay behind me, out of sight and will not take part unless I am in trouble."

Pablo nodded and smiled as he replied, "I promise."

They lay down on the rocky ground, sharing Pablo's heavy wool blanket. Pablo was asleep quickly, his breathing deep and regular. Tye lay thinking of a lot of things: Rebecca and the baby was at the top of the list followed by Todd and wondering how he was, and finally, just how he planned to get even with Alvarez and his men and still accomplish what he started out to do which was to find Zach. With so much on his mind it was impossible to sort things out and besides, after the events of today he was exhausted. He fell asleep.

Dawn came too soon as it always does when you are tired, but the scout had things to do, so he was up and doing them. After a quick breakfast of cold tortillas and water, he left Pablo in camp and headed to the village. He needed to see what Alvarez had his men doing.

The first thing he did before waking Pablo was clean the Henry rifle he had taken from the guard. He had never seen a gun so dirty. It was now in perfect working order and fully loaded with thirteen bullets.

It was full light when he settled behind some sage and cedars seventy yards from the stables. The first thing he saw was Sandy.

"Thank God he is okay," Tye thought. *"Somehow, I will get him tonight."* His thoughts were interrupted by two Mexicans on horses leaving the village, rifles lying across their thighs. As they rode, they were looking toward the hills, obviously looking for something or someone. Tye glanced back at the village and saw a man hanging from a tree by his neck.

"Damn! That's the man who was guarding me last night." He was shocked at the cruelty of some men. He couldn't believe the man was hung just because he was struck from behind. *"A man that would do that needs to be served some of his own medicine."*

Tye slipped over the rim and down the other side. He had an idea those two were going to go down the trail a ways and hide, waiting to see if he showed himself and finish what they had started yesterday. He knew the trail was crooked and almost doubled back before heading east toward Pablo's village. He could get ahead and wait for them along the trail. He never had ambushed any man, but this was different. There were ten or so of them and he had to whittle them down some.

An hour later he was behind a cedar about five yards off the trail. He had checked for fresh hoof prints and found none. They had stopped and hid somewhere between here and the village or they were still coming, just in no hurry.

Tye felt of his head which stilled seeped a little blood and then at his chaffed wrists. He had been hidden no more than five minutes when he heard a horse whinny. He cocked the Henry.

"*It has begun,*" he thought to himself. "*After this there will be no turning back.*" He could not see the men but he knew they were very close. He could hear them talking. Taking a deep breath he stepped from behind the cedars as they came into view and yelled.

"YOU HOMBRES LOOKING FOR ME?" His sudden appearance startled both men and the horses. One horse reared, throwing its rider, but the other man quickly got control of his mount and was bringing his rifle up when Tye's bullet hit him in the forehead. Even though the Henry was not known for power and distance, at twenty feet the bullet exploded out the back of the man's head spewing blood, bone, and brain- matter. The other man had lost his rifle when he fell from his rearing horse. Tye walked to him, holding the barrel of the Henry pointed toward the bandit's chest.

He had no intention of killing this man unless he was forced to. He wanted him to deliver a message, but he did not want this man to have a chance to shoot him later. He thought about it for a minute and decided what he would do. He had a reputation as being part Apache so he would play the part now to the fullest.

~~

At Fort Clark things were returning to normal. Rebecca woke up feeling well, no pain at all. The post surgeon had visited and said she could go home. Buff and Todd had spent the night with her in the hospital and they were both asleep. Rebecca sat in the chair on the porch drinking coffee. She loved to sit out here in the mornings. There was always so much to see and hear. The birds sat in the oaks along the creek chatting and there were always some small animals like coons, possums, and squirrels frolicking along the creek. Their house was on the southern edge of the fort and this area of the creek did not receive the foot traffic that the other parts did. She figured that was why there were always things to see.

This was also her favorite time to think about things. Things like how much she loved Tye and how he was looking forward to the baby. She thought of how much the O'Malley's had meant to her since her parents had been killed by the Comanche two years ago. She appreciated so much the officer's wives giving her all the baby gifts. It was not like in a city where they could go buy them. Everything was hand-made, and made well. The baby bed made by Sergeant O'Malley was her favorite. Everyone had been surprised by the quality of the work because he had never made anything like that before. Sitting there, she also counted her blessings that she had met Tye and fallen in love. She could have met another man that might have taken her to live alone on a farm or ranch. She admired the women who lived in this land away from other people and not seeing anyone for days on end except for family. She did not think she was strong enough to live each day like that knowing that any minute bandits or Apaches could come. She loved Fort Clark and its beauty. It was beautiful along the creek compared to the barren, arid land that surrounded it for more than a hundred miles in every direction. She was very content with her life right now and knew with the coming of the baby, would get even better.

Gary McMillan

Chapter Nineteen

Tye tied the dead man across the saddle of his horse. He tied the other man's hands behind his back, blindfolded him with his own kerchief, and tied a rope around the man's neck. Tye led them to where he and Pablo had spent the night. Tye explained to Pablo what had happened and that he was sending this man back with a message, but he did not want to have to worry about the man shooting him later. To Pablo's horror he laid the man's hand on a rock and using the butt of the rifle, smashed his right hand and then with the man screaming in pain and begging him not to, mashed the left.

When the man quieted down in a few minutes to only a whimper, Tye had Pablo give him a message to give Alvarez. The message was simple and to the point. Pablo translated the message in Spanish so the man could understand.

"I came here to find Zach Robertson who almost beat my fourteen year old nephew to death just to steal his horse. For no reason, you tried to have me killed. Now, the choice is yours. You can leave and give me Zach or stay and die."

After helping the injured man on his horse and sending him back to the village, Tye knew he had some explaining to do to

249

Pablo. He knew the man had been shocked at what he had just done.

"Why did you do that to that man?" Pablo asked before he could explain.

"Sit down for a minute Pablo," he said. "I told you it was going to get nasty around here. That, and I did not want to see you hurt, is why I wanted you to go back to your village yesterday. When dealing with men like Alvarez, the only thing they understand is violence. I did not want to kill that man but I didn't want him to kill me later if I let him go. His hands will be okay in a few weeks."

He sat down by his friend. "I am not a man looking for trouble, but when it comes my way, I won't back down from it. I've learned one thing over the years, Pablo. To survive, you have to fight like those who are trying to kill you: be just as vicious as they are. I have seen men killed by men they let live for one reason or another. That is not going to happen to me. Alvarez has his warning. What happens now is up to him. If you want to stay you are welcome, but if you stay, be prepared to defend yourself and do things you never thought you would do."

Pablo understood what Tye was saying and guessed what he had seen his friend do to that bandit was more humane than to kill him. He had seen things worse done to his villagers by men like Alvarez from time to time. He figured the men, women, and children of this village were seeing that from Alvarez and his men now.

"I understand why you did that, Tye. I also know that if these men are not stopped they will eventually come to my village and maybe hurt my children and my wife. That is the way men like that are. They take advantage of the ones that are weak, like the village people."

"The people of your village, and these villagers here are not weak, Pablo. They just have different values than those men. It takes more of a man to raise, work, and support a family than to do what those men do which is to take what men like you and your friends work for. They are worthless pieces of horse shit and don't deserve to live among honest folks like you. I told you once that I would help you and your village. In a round about way, by getting rid of Alvarez may do that." He put his hand on Pablo's shoulder. "You are my friend Pablo and if you go, you will still be my friend."

Pablo stood up and Tye figured he was leaving. Pablo stuck out his chest. "What is your plan of attack so I can help?"

"You're staying?"

"Of course I am. You are my friend and friends do not abandon each other and besides, like you said a minute ago, those men may be in my village next."

Tye was elated, but he knew he should not have been. His friend had never been in a fight like he was headed toward. Sure, he had knocked that guard out last night, but there is a big difference in knocking a man out and killing a man. I will need him to watch my back and any hesitation on his part could get both of us killed.

"Are you sure, Pablo? Are you absolute sure, because once we start, there will be no turning back?" Pablo nodded his head.

Tye shook his hand. "Good. Now this is what we are going to do tonight."

~~

Alvarez was livid. He cursed in Spanish and he cursed in English. He then cursed in a language neither he nor his men understood. Finally, when he could think of no other foul words to say, he sat down at the table in the cantina and with his hand, knocked glasses, bottles and plates across the room. His men backed away. They had seen what he had done before when he was mad, but no one had ever seen him this mad. There was no telling what he would do or who he would kill in this frame of mind.

"Lupe…come here and sit with me. The rest of you, get out." The men hurried out, glad to be away from him, even if for a short time. Lupe sat down. He was the one man who could calm Alvarez down and speak to him in a tone he understood.

Lupe motioned to the fat lady to bring them a bottle and two glasses. When she left, he poured both a drink and pushed the glass in front of Alvarez. "Drink my friend. We will talk." They both downed their tequila in one quick gulp.

Alvarez leaned back in his chair, both hands resting on the edge of the table. "I am going to kill this scout. I should have done it yesterday when you brought him to me. I wanted to wait until he was awake so he could see who was killing him. That was my mistake. I won't make it again." Lupe poured them another shot and they again downed them. "How many men do we have?"

"We had thirteen not counting you and me. One was hung, the scout killed one and one is injured. Now, counting me and you, we have twelve that can fight."

"He says he is going to kill all of us. To do that, he will have to come to us. Take four of our men and post them as sentries around the village tonight. Have them relieved every two hours so they can stay alert. You tell them that this man is like an Apache and can kill them before they even know he is there, so they damn well better stay sharp."

"It will be done." Lupe started out the door then stopped, turning back he asked. "What about your friend, Zach?"

"He brought this on us. I will deal with him when this is over."

~~

"The first thing I am going to do is go into the village tonight and do what damage I can do without being seen," Tye said to Pablo. He took a stick and started making 'X's in the dirt. One marked the cantina, one the shed he had been held in, one was the stables and the last one was a hill just on the outskirts of town, close to the stables. It was the hill he had been on earlier and knew it had good cover and a good field of fire. "This is where I want you to be watching the town…and my back from. I know how men like this think. He will expect us to bring the fight to him and he will have sentries out tonight. We will hit them after midnight when they may get a little careless. In the mean time, let's get some food in our bellies and some rest."

Pablo was concerned. "Do you think that is wise…to go into the village?"

"They tried to kill me, Pablo. For no damn reason, they bushwhacked me. I am going to give them some of their own medicine. They are going to be hit and never see it coming. I've never started a fight in my life, but I've ended a few and this is one I'm going to end. I'm going to fight, but it's going to be on my terms…my way. They can stay and maybe die or they can give me Zach, leave this village and live."

~~

It had only been two days, but Zach was sick of the cabin. He wanted something to drink and there was nothing here. He had walked the area and was impressed with the sight. He was two or three thousand feet higher here than in the village and the nights were a lot cooler and the days not quite so warm.

He had seen no use in him coming up here in the first place. No soldiers were going to be coming into Mexico and risk the possible political backlash if caught. There was no reason for that damn scout to come just because he beat the hell out of a kid. Besides, how in hell could anyone know who he was? The kid might be able to describe him but no one would be able to put a name to the description. He would wait one more day and then go back, "I don't care what that ass Alvarez thinks," he mumbled.

~~

The sun had set and it was full dark as Tye and Pablo sat in their camp. Tye could tell Pablo was nervous because he was not talking, just sitting there. Being nervous was normal. I'm nervous

255

myself so why worry about my friend. Being nervous and being scared are two very different things. Being nervous can keep a man sharp, alert to things going on around him. Being scared could hinder one's thinking and make him hesitate. I hope Pablo is just nervous.

Tye stood up and Pablo did the same. "Is it time?"

Tye nodded. "It will take us an hour or so to get you in position, and another hour for me to figure out where the sentries are." He wished he had a smoke but the makings were in his saddle bags somewhere in the village so that would have to wait awhile. "You ready?" Tye said giving Pablo his most confident smile possible.

"Let's go." Pablo answered.

Chapter Twenty

It was midnight when Tye had Pablo where he wanted him on the side of the hill overlooking the village. He instructed him not to move or make any noise. It was damn dark with a low cloud cover blocking any light from the stars and the new moon. Tye moved slowly down the hill, careful not to loosen any rocks. He stopped and let his eyes scan the buildings and areas in between looking for the sentries.

As he watched, a match flared as one of the men actually lit a smoke. Tye could see the red glow from the tip when the man inhaled. *"That's one, now to find the others. I figure there will be three or four."* He watched for ten more minutes and saw no one. He mentally marked the spot where he saw the cigarette flare up, and quietly made his way there. The soft-soled Apache boots he wore made no sound.

He held a pistol in his left hand and the knife he had taken from the guard in his right. As he moved ever so slowly to where he saw the glow of the cigarette, he searched the windows and alleyways for the other guards.

When he was a few feet from the man with the cigarette, he hesitated long enough to take one more look around. Hearing and seeing nothing, he was poised to quickly take the three or four steps needed to take the guard down. He raised his right foot to take that first step, but stopped, his foot hanging in mid air. He had heard a noise above him. Slowly looking up, he saw a rifle protruding from the window on the second floor above him. The guard laying the rifle on the wooden window seal had made the noise.

Slipping back in the shadows, he backed along the wall until he found the door. Praying the door's hinges didn't squeak, he slowly opened it, quickly stepped in, and closed the door behind him. His eyes, already accustomed to the dark quickly scanned the room.

Thankfully, it was empty and he quickly made his way to the stairs. Carefully, he took the steps of the stairs one at a time and not putting all his weight down until he was sure the step did not make any creaking noise, he headed up. Reaching the top, he quickly found the room where he figured the sentry was and lightly scratched on the door, and then listened, his knife held low, the edge up ready to strike. Not hearing anything he repeated the scratching, this time a little louder. He heard footsteps coming toward the door and he tensed, ready to strike. The door opened inward. He rushed in and brought his blade up slashing the man's throat. He grabbed the rifle as the man released his grip on it to grab his throat. Blood sprayed and ran between his fingers, and as he began to fall, Tye grabbed him. The only noise was a gurgling sound. Tye laid him on the floor and stepped out of the room and shut the door.

He backtracked down the stairs and opening the door, stepped out into the quiet street and listened. All was quiet so he moved again toward the stupid sentry that was still puffing on the cigarette; the glow leading Tye to him like a beacon. Tye took the pistol from his waist behind his back. When he was close enough he took two quick steps and from behind the guard, struck him above the ear with the butt of the heavy Colt. The guard dropped like a rock to the ground. Tye hit the man hard enough to split his skull, but didn't bother to check to see if the man was dead or alive. Tye picked up the rifle and the bandoleer from around the man's chest. He quickly retraced his steps to the edge of the village, and in a crouch, quickly moved up the hill where Pablo was watching.

Pablo was anxious to hear what had happened. "What happened?" he asked.

"There's one maybe two that won't be taking advantage of the village people any more."

"One or two?"

"Yeah, I killed one outright and hit the other hard enough with the butt of my pistol to kill him, but I don't know if he died or not. If he didn't, we won't have to worry about him for awhile.

Let's get back to camp and wait and see what happens when they find them."

"Why don't we wait here and see."

"I thought about that, but there are drawbacks by staying here. I think Alvarez will go crazy mad. He's smart enough to know that I would not still be in the village. This hill is the most likely place to launch an attack from, so he would send his men rushing up the hill to find us. Come daylight, he will fan his men out in the countryside to find me. I had rather meet them out here in the hills where we can move around, than be trapped on the hill or in the village.

"We have guns and bullets. We can fight them from here."

"Yes, we do, but hitting a man that is moving is tough and twice as tough in the dark. They would probably overrun us. The smart thing is to leave and let him rant and rave and then when things have settled down some, we'll finish things…if he stays. The choice is still his."

Pablo agreed with Tye's plan and they left the hill, hurrying in the dark back to their camp.

About an hour after Tye and Pablo left the hill, an angry Alvarez was cursing everyone and everything. He chastised the other two guards and then slapped them across the face for not seeing the scout. The normally cool and in control boss that his men knew, was gone. He had the men fanning out in the hills around the village trying to find the scout, but even in the state of mind he was now in, he knew his men wouldn't find him. He walked to the cantina, kicked the door in, and went behind the bar grabbing a bottle of tequila and sat down at a table. He downed three quick shots and was pouring a fourth when Lupe walked in.

"No sign of the scout anywhere," he said.

Alvarez gave a slight nod and then downed his fourth drink. "I want him found, Lupe. I want the gringo bastard dead. At first light, I want the men in three groups and search the areas south, east, and north of the village for two miles and I want a thorough search, not a half-assed one."

"What about west?"

"I don't think he came from the west. That would mean he came from deeper in Mexico. I'm betting he came in a direct line from Texas into this village. That means he is probably camped east of here. I would like you to take that direction, find him and finished what you started." He shook his head and poured himself another drink. "I should have killed him when you brought him in." He stood up and put his hand on his friends shoulder. "He's dangerous Lupe. Don't under estimate his abilities and get yourself killed."

Lupe walked outside the cantina and gathered the men around him. He explained what they were going to do. It was over two hours till first light, so he told them to get some rest.

A mile east of the village Tye lay on the ground, staring at the night sky which was just beginning to show the first signs of gray. He had not gone to sleep, but lay there, making plans for what he and Pablo should do at daylight. He knew the Mexicans would be scouring the country side and would be coming from the direction of the village.

He decided the best plan was the simplest, but it had always worked, especially when the men attacking were looking for blood and maybe not thinking as clear as normal. That reasoning was why he always tried to stay calm in all situations.

He woke Pablo up and explained what they would do.

"Do you think they would be foolish enough to fall for that?"

"It always worked for me."

"How many times have you used it?"

Tye laughed. "Once."

"ONCE," Pablo said almost shouting. The smiled and shrugged, "Maybe it will work twice."

After building a small fire they took brush and small limbs and tucked them under the blanket to look like a man sleeping. They placed Tye's hat and Pablo's sombrero as if they were lying across the faces of the sleeping men. Pablo's donkey was hidden well away from the camp. Hopefully the bandits would fall for the old trick and come into the camp bunched together. That was the plan, but Tye was a little apprehensive as to whether it would work or not. If it didn't, they would put plan "B" into action which was pretty simple... run like hell away from there due east toward Texas and regroup.

Tye placed Pablo about forty yards up a slope on the east side of the camp. He was well hidden and Tye showed him an escape route if needed where he could leave without being seen. Tye took up a position on the same slope but farther to Pablo's right. He figured it would be about an hour before the bandits found the camp. The fire had burned down and was now leaving a small trail of smoke that, with no early morning breeze, spiraled almost straight up making it easily visible.

Tye was caught by surprise when he saw the man approaching the camp after only fifteen minutes of waiting. He was on foot and Tye quickly scanned the area for others. He saw two coming from the other side of camp. The three men were thirty feet from the supposedly sleeping scout when a forth man appeared. He was fifty yards away and motioned for the men to back off, but it was too late. One of the men fired into the blankets, and then the other two followed suit. Tye opened up with his Henry and the first two shots took down the two men doing the shooting and as he swung the barrel to where the third man was, he saw him fall, clutching his chest. Tye swung the gun and fired at the fourth man. He knocked the man down only to see him crawl behind a clump of thick sage. He fired five shots into the brush, spacing the shots a little ways apart from one end to the other. He signaled Pablo to stay where he was. As was his custom, he quickly replaced the spent shells. It was something his pa had always been adamant about.

"Keep you gun loaded at all times."

He watched the brush where the man had crawled while he replaced the spent shell. He waited for about five minutes before carefully approaching the stand of sage. He was taking one slow step at a time and had the Henry against his shoulder, sighting down the barrel as he walked. The man was gone but he did find blood on a limb about four foot off the ground and some more on the ground. Tye looked at the tracks and the blood and thought, *"From where the blood is on the limb I figure I hit him in the shoulder. It was probably only a scratch since there isn't much on the ground."*

He turned and signaled Pablo to go into the camp. He had looked at the three men that were down, none moved, so he figured they were dead. He walked down the slope to the camp and met Pablo. Tye immediately saw that his Mexican friend was not well. He looked a little sick.

"You okay Pablo?" Pablo did not answer but let the rifle fall from his hands and sat down. Tye knew what was wrong and had expected it. He had been surprised the little man had fired the rifle in the first place.

"Tye sat down and put his arm around his friend. "I know how you feel Pablo. It hurts when you kill a man, especially the first time. I want to thank you for your help and for saving me from some serious pain from that sonofabitch yesterday. Now, I want you to get on your donkey and go home. Go back to your wife and kids. When I am though here, I will stop in your village and we will talk." He stood up and grabbed Pablo by the shoulder and lifted him to his feet. "Now go." He gently pushed him toward where the donkey was hidden. Pablo looked over his shoulder, a great sadness showing on his face. He waved once and disappeared into the bush. Tye gathered his blanket and hat, checked the dead men for anything he could use and left, moving north to get on the other side of the village.

Pablo was hurting inside. He was hurt that he could no longer help his friend, but killing that man hurt more than he could stand. It was against everything he believed and he was thankful it happened away from his village because they would never know. Tye was right when he said it hurt to take a life and it did, more than he expected. He prayed that God would look over his friend. He prayed that God would forgive him for what he had done. He stopped and started to go back, but when he looked, his friend was gone.

~~

Alvarez looked up from his drink as his man, Lupe, stumbled into the cantina with help from another man.

Jumping up he hollered, "WHAT HAPPENED?" He hurried over to help his friend to a chair. He turned and screamed at the woman that ran the cantina. "GET ME SOME TOWELS AND HOT WATER." He turned back to Lupe and knelt down in front of the wounded man. "Tell me what happened."

Lupe told the story with a few pauses as he grimaced each time a new wave of pain swept through him. He was hit in the right shoulder and the bullet had gone through clean. Alvarez ripped his friend's shirt off and looked at the wound. There was a small purple hole in front with little blood, but where the bullet exited in the back was a hole as big as a twenty dollar gold piece and a lot of blood.

The fat woman returned with towels and hot water. Alvarez stood up and grabbed her arm. "Doctor his wound woman."

He walked back to his table and sat down and downed his drink he had poured earlier. "Damn him…damn that stinking gringo to hell," he mumbled.

Gary McMillan

Chapter Twenty One

Tye moved quickly, but not carelessly, through the gulleys, brush, and cactus. He watched for trouble every step of the way. He figured he had traveled a half mile when he stopped to listen and study the lay of the land in front of him. He had been trotting in the sandy bottom of a dry creek that ran in the direction he wanted to go. He decided he would stay in the creek for now. At least he made no noise when he moved in the sand.

After a short rest, he was on the move again. He carried the Henry in his right hand as he jogged. He ran around a bend in the creek and unexpectedly, found himself face to face with three Mexicans. The three men were as surprised as he was, but reacted a little slower. Tye crabbed to the right and brought the Henry into play, firing as fast as he could. He saw the closest man take a bullet square in the brisket. His second or third shot hit the second man, striking him in the stomach. He doubled over clutching his belly. Tye swung his rifle toward the third man and as he squeezed the trigger, he saw the smoke of the man's pistol. Tye felt a sudden burning sensation on his left upper arm and at the same time saw the man drop his pistol and grab his shoulder. Tye took three quick steps and struck the wounded man on the top of the head with the butt of his Henry, crushing the man's sombrero. He did an about face and had the rifle ready to fire as he checked the other two. One was obviously dead; the one shot in the belly didn't have long to live. Tye kicked the wounded man's rifle away from him and then took his pistol from its holster and threw it into the brush. He picked up both men's rifles and broke the butts on the rocks, rendering them useless.

He checked his shoulder, finding a lot of blood running down his arm. The bullet had cut a quarter inch deep gash across his upper arm. It wasn't serious, but it was going to be pretty damn painful. Doctoring it though would have to wait awhile. Those shots would bring some men and he wasn't going to be here to welcome them.

Alvarez leaped to his feet at the sound of the shots thinking, *"They got that gringo bastard. They got him."* He ran outside the cantina and followed two of his men who were headed out of the village on the north side. They met three more that had been searching the hills.

"Where did the shots come from?" He asked grabbing one of his men by the arm. "Where?' he repeated.

"Just over this hill, I think." They all ran up the hill and each man stopped short of the top. They were going to take a look before they showed themselves. One man dropped behind some brush and took a look. A few seconds later he stood up and motioned for the rest to come. They started down the other side and saw two men lying on the ground and a third sitting up, his back against a big boulder.

Alvarez, looking at his dead men lying on the ground and the one wounded, he looked at the hills and screamed, "DAMN YOU WATKINS." He shook his fist at the hills. "DAMN YOU TO HELL." He looked back at the men on the ground and shook his head. He had more damn men dead and wounded than he had healthy.

"What kind of a man is this? I knew the scout was good but this bordered on the ridiculous," he thought to himself. *"These men he had killed and wounded were fighting men, not untested amateurs."* He looked at the men standing before him." Pick up these men and bring them back to the village."

He headed back alone, nervous for the first time in many years. As he walked, he looked at the hills, looked behind him, he looked everywhere, expecting to see the scout at any time pointing a rifle at him. It wasn't a good feeling.

~~

Thirty minutes and a mile or so away from where he met the three outlaws, Tye sat down by a small pool, formed by a spring that bubbled out of the side of a cliff. He washed the wound on his shoulder the best he could with the clear, cool water. The blood had almost stopped and the wound only hurt when his heart beat. He had nothing to bandage it with to help keep it clean. Unless he could get some rotgut to pour on it, he knew it was going to become infected and then hurt more than it did now.

"*I'll have to go into the village tonight and get some whiskey. There's no way to keep it from getting worse unless I do. I...*" his thoughts were interrupted by the sound of hooves striking the rocky ground. He quickly slipped into the brush and waited to see who was coming. He didn't think it was one of the outlaws because by the sound of the horses, the rider was coming from the northwest, heading toward the village not from it. Listening to the clamor the hooves were making, he figured there were two horses.

Zach Robertson had his fill of the cabin. He wanted a woman and he wanted some whiskey, neither of which he had at the cabin. He rode looking straight ahead, completely unaware of the events that had taken place at the village. The only thing on his mind was a bottle and a woman. He was leading the horse he had taken from the kid and intended to try and sell it to Alvarez. He had tried to saddle him at the cabin and was knocked down by the damn, crazy animal.

Tye saw the man and recognized the horse trailing behind him even though he was almost a hundred yards away. The man fit the description he had been given by the man at the saloon in

Brackettville. He felt his stomach tightened and his heart began pounding.

"That's him…that's the sonofabitch Robertson that beat Todd." It would be an easy shot for a man of Tye's ability and he raised the rifle to his shoulder and sighted down the barrel. He was squeezing the trigger when the reality of what he was about to do struck him. As much as he hated the man, he could not just shoot a man from ambush. He lowered the rifle and started trotting toward the man and horses. He was slightly behind them. The man was obviously not paying any attention to his surroundings and had not seen him, but he figured the horses would soon enough.

He was fifty yards behind the man when he saw him suddenly pull up. Tye stopped, stepped behind some thick cedars to watch and see what the man saw that made him stop. A few seconds later two Mexicans appeared in front of Zach. They had come out of the brush and began having a heated discussion with Zach. He could only pick up some of the words, but it sounded like they were telling Zach some of their friends were dead and blaming it on him. Zach was looking in all directions while they spoke to him. He was obviously looking to see if he was in the rifle sights of this crazy scout.

One of the men left and then came back in a couple minutes with his and the other man's horses. Mounted, they followed Zach toward the village. Zach's mind was racing now and he was a little bit more than nervous. The two Mexicans had told him that Alvarez was madder than hell at him for bringing the gringo to his village and he now knew for a fact that Watkins was a little more than chafed or he would not have followed him this far into Mexico. He was perplexed as to why the scout had followed him just because he beat up a kid and stole a horse.

"*Hell,*" he thought, *"you'd think that damn kid was his son or some other relative.*"

Alvarez was sitting in the shade of the porch of the cantina when the three men rode into town. He was on his feet immediately when he saw Zach. He stepped down off the porch and pretended to be glad to see him.

"Well Zach," he said. "This is a surprise. I wasn't expecting to see you for a couple more days." He had a forced smile spread across his face. "Get down," Alvarez said, and then repeated what he said, smiling even more. "Get down and let's talk."

This was not what Zach expected and it kind of threw him off some. His feeble brain was trying to figure out why Alvarez was being so friendly when the two men had just told him how upset he was. He had his hand resting on his thigh close to his gun when he rode in. He relaxed some and put his hands on the pommel of the saddle and looked at Alvarez.

"Heard you had some trouble?"

"A little but it's over. We caught him." The two Mexican bandits looked at each other questionably. This was news to them because just ten minutes ago the gringo was still loose. One looked at Alvarez and started to speak, but stopped when Alvarez gave him a look the outlaw gives just before he kills someone. The man said nothing. Zach dismounted and followed Alavarez into the cantina.

Walking into the cantina from the bright sun into the gloomy, dimly lit room, it took a couple of seconds for his eyes to adjust. When they did, he clearly saw Alvarez standing in front of him, the smile gone and holding a gun that was pointed directly at Zach's stomach.

"Sit." Alvarez growled, and kicked a chair at Zach. One of the men reacted quickly and grabbed Zach's arms from behind. He turned his head when he got a whiff of the odor coming from the gringo. The other man took Zach's pistol from its holster and the Bowie from the sheath on the belt from the left side.

"WHAT'S THIS ALL ABOUT?" Zach demanded.

Alvarez was ready to kill him but held off squeezing the trigger. "What it is all about, he asks," Alvarez said looking at his men. He laughed loud…a deep laugh that Zach thought had a different meaning than being funny. Zach could see the fury in his expression when Alvarez answered. "I'll tell you what it is about you gringo bastard. I have six or seven men dead and three more injured because you had that stinking scout, Tye Watkins, following you to my village. Because of you I have no gang any more." He slapped Zach so hard it knocked the big man out of the chair. Zach jumped to his feet and started to step toward Alvarez when he heard the distinct sound of a pistol being cocked. He stopped dead in his tracks; a fury like he had not felt in a long time rose up inside and almost overrode the fact that he was a twitch of a finger from death. He stood there like a statue, staring at this man that until a minute ago was his only friend in the whole damn world.

"I…I had no idea he would follow me here over a kid and a stolen horse."

"I've a feeling there's more to it than that." Alvarez said motioning with the pistol for Zach to sit. After the man sat down, Alvarez sat down at the table and laid his pistol on the table in front of him. A quick glance from Zach showed the man's hand close to the gun. There was a long moment of silence except the drumming noise of the outlaw's fingers on the table.

~~

Tye sat on the hill he and Pablo had been on last night. He was well hidden, but he could see what was going on in the village. He saw Zach and Alvarez go into the cantina followed by the other two outlaws. He did not know what was going on, but he could not believe that Alvarez could be happy with Zach. It was because of Zach that he was here, and he figured the boss man was smart enough to put two and two together and come up with the fact that all his problems could be traced to Zach. As he watched the events taking place below, he was startled by a voice coming from behind him. Turning his head slowly, he looked back up the hill and saw two men coming down the slope. They were engaged in some serious talk and not paying attention or they probably would have already seen the scout. Tye saw that if they didn't change course they would pass within ten feet of where he lay hidden and there would no way they could not miss seeing him. He was in a fix and he knew it. He had his back to them and to fire he had to twist his body around. They would see him the instant he moved giving them the advantage. As he pondered what to do, they suddenly veered a little to their right which would make their path be a few feet, maybe fifteen or twenty to Tye's right. They would still see him but not as quickly as they would have coming down directly behind him. Tye shifted his feet to get into position to attack as soon as they saw him. He took a quick glance down the slope to the village and saw no one but a few of the villagers moving about. That encouraged him some.

Second Chance

"Maybe I can get one with the Bowie and then get the drop on the other and take him out quietly. A shot will have the rest of the men up here in a few seconds like a bunch of hungry wolves."

He reached behind him and pulled the Bowie he had taken from the sentry and flipped it around in his hand. He held the tip of the blade between his thumb and index finger, the handle in the air.. He waited until the men were almost even with him and about fifteen feet away. He quickly stood up. "You two looking for me."

The reaction was immediate, just as he would expect from battle tested men. They both spun to their left toward the voice and were beginning to bring their rifles up as the Bowie spun through the air toward them, the late evening sun's rays shimmering off the blade.

Chapter Twenty Two

The Bowie in the hand of someone who knows how to handle one can be a very dangerous and lethal weapon. Tye had been taught by the best-his pa. The Bowie buried itself in the chest of the man nearest to him. The scout switched the Henry from his left to his right hand and was bringing the barrel up just as the blade struck the bandit. The second man, startled by the knife sticking from his friend's chest was an instant slow in bringing his gun to bear on Tye. Tye fired and saw a puff of dust from the man's dirty shirt when the bullet slammed into his chest. Tye took another quick look below and cursed when he saw two men that had apparently come out of the cantina. One was pointing up the hill. Tye ran toward the crest of the hill. He ran a zig zag course using the cedars and sage the best he could to shield him as the two men fired their rifles as fast as they could pull the trigger and chamber another round. Bullets hit rocks and cedars all around him.

As he ran he felt something like a fist hit him in his upper right leg. His leg betrayed him and he went down hard with more bullets splattering rock fragments and dirt in his face. When the shock of what happened passed he realized he had been hit in the back of his leg, about midway between his knee and butt. The pain set in as he crawled behind some big boulders that lay in a stand of cedars. He was hidden from

the guns below and took a minute to catch his breath and look at the wound. He could hear shouts from below and knew more men were coming. It was going to be painful to try and walk, never mind run.

"Tye, you've got yourself in one hell of a fix. You can't run, they know where you are, and there's a lot more of them than you."

Looking at the wound he was thankful it had not been a direct hit but instead, had sliced a deep furrow in the muscle of his thigh. Always thinking ahead and being the optimist he was, he was glad it was on the outside of his leg and not the inside. Being on the inside would make it hard to sit a saddle-that is if he ever as the chance to sit a saddle again.

He took a look over the top of the boulder he was behind and saw four men making their way up the slope.

"I'm sure Alvarez has a man or two on the other side of this hill in case I make a run for it." He smiled at that thought despite his situation. *"It would be nice if I could make a run for it. He looked around and despite his wounds and being surrounded; he was in a pretty good defensive position. I might as well lower the odds some. He laid the rifle across the boulder and centered the*

'V' of the sights on the barrel on the closest man's chest which was about forty yards from him. Shooting uphill or downhill can be tricky sometimes, but at forty yards, it should be no problem. He slowly put pressure on the trigger.

Below, Alvarez was moving up the hill with his men. The two men saw Watkins hit and go down, but no one knew how hard he was hit or if he was alive or dead. Alvarez thought.

"If there is a God above, He will let him be alive. I want him alive so I can see the great scout squirm and beg for mercy before I kill him." He had lost more than enough men to this man so he told his men to take their time and be damn careful. He had his best rifleman on the other side of the hill to make sure Watkins didn't escape that way.

~~

Two miles to the east, a lone rider was heading for the little village. He was tired and his horse had seen better days. Two days riding with no rest or sleep would do that to man and beast. The rider had a purpose for pushing himself and his mount this hard; he had a friend that could be in trouble, according to the Mexican named Pablo in the last village he passed through.

He was thankful his quest was almost over because his horse could not go another five miles. The rider was not a big man, but if one looked close, he could quickly tell he could be a dangerous man, a man that could take care of himself. He wore knee high Apache style moccasin boots with a ten inch Bowie in a sheath in his right boot. He had a tomahawk stuck in his belt on his left side and a Navy Colt in the holster on his right hip. Resting across his thighs, his right hand holding the butt laid a thirteen shot repeating Henry rifle. An old single shot big bore Sharps rested in the saddle scabbard he would use for long distance shooting.

As tired as he was his eyes never quit moving as they moved along the trail. He saw everything in front and both sides of the canyon the trail cut through. He reached down and patted his mount on the neck. "It won't be long now boy." He said. "Just give me a couple more miles and you can rest and have all the grain you want." The rider sat up straight and a couple bones in his back popped. He had been slouched over too long.

Dan August had left Fort Clark as soon as he had heard about Tye leaving.. Dan was one of Tye's most trusted scouts and friends and he was here to pay back all the times Tye had helped him. Tye had pulled his butt out of the fire more than once the last two years and he had waited for the opportunity to return the favor. From what Pablo had told him Tye was facing, he hoped he was not too late.

He reined his horse in to listen. The breeze was in his face and he thought he heard what sounded like rifle fire.

~~

Tye put more pressure on the trigger and the gun bucked against his shoulder. The man he aimed at clutched his chest and fell into a patch of cactus. The other men dropped out of sight immediately. *"That should keep their heads down for awhile and give me time to think of a way out of this."* He glanced over his shoulder to see if anyone was coming over the hill. Seeing no one, he moved a little to his right so a large boulder would be between him and the crest of the hill and keep him out of sight if someone did.

He was tired, his shoulder burned, and now his leg was throbbing. He was hungry and thirsty and had neither food nor water and he was trapped on the side of a hill. *"What a great day,"* he thought. Despite of his plight he had to laugh. He ducked as several bullets came whistling through the cedars and ricocheting off the rocks.

Dan had arrived in the village and the first thing he saw brought a smile to his face. Laid out on the porch of the cantina were the bodies of seven Mexican bandits. Another man sat in a chair, his arm in a sling, eyeing him suspiciously. Dan noticed the man's rifle was 'accidentally' pointed in his general direction.

"You speak English?" Dan asked.

"Enough," answered Lupe, his finger resting close to the trigger.

"What happened?" Dan asked, nodding toward the bodies. He knew Tye had a hand in the deaths and in this man's wound, but no one needed to know about his knowing Tye…not yet anyway.

"A gringo like you did it."

"One man did this?"

"That man is the head scout at Fort Clark."

"You mean Tye Watkins?" The man nodded, and Dan said. "What in the hell is the Chief of Scouts at Fort Clark doing over here in Mexico."

Lupe shrugged his shoulders. Dan noticed his hand moved a little farther away from the trigger and the barrel lowered a little. Then the Mexican said. "We will know why soon. He is trapped on the slope there." He nodded toward the hill whose slope flattened out at the edge of town.

Dan looked at the slope and it didn't take him long to figure where Tye was probably hidden. Not wanting the man to think he was too interested in the man on the hill he looked around at the buildings around him. "That his horse there with the U.S. Army brand on it?" Dan asked nodding toward the two horses at the hitching rail.

"No. Those belong to that stupid gringo that Tye followed here, Zach Robertson."

"Big feller, always wears a stinking Buffalo robe?"

The rifle came back up. "You a friend of his?" His hand moved back to the trigger.

"Nope. Don't even know the man, but I was through Brackettville a couple days ago and the town was talking about this feller, Zach that beat the hell out of a fourteen year old kid and stole a good looking horse. He was said to be riding a black horse with a blaze on his face like the one standing next to the one with the army brand. They said Watkins was furious and left the fort swearing to track the man down and kill him. Can't say I blame the scout. I have no use for a piece of dung that would do that to a kid."

Dan saw the gun lowered some and the Mexican seem to relax. He forced a smile and asked. "Can a thirsty man get a drink in there?"

Lupe nodded and motioned with his head it was okay to go in. Dan dismounted, wrapped his reins around the rail, and taking his Henry out of the scabbard walked by Lupe into the cantina. Looking around he saw no one except a heavy set woman behind the bar. "You speak English?" he asked. She shook her head. Dan made a motion with his hand indicating he wanted a drink. She nodded. He sat at a table to where he could see the hill through the window. He saw three men that were twenty or so yards up the slope. One was a white man wearing a heavy robe. He figured that was Zach.

He downed the drink the woman had set on the table along with a bottle. He poured himself another. He sat there looking out the window, trying to figure a plan of action to help his friend.

Chapter Twenty Three

Dan took another look around the cantina. On the table a few feet from where he sat were some familiar weapons; a Navy Colt resting in a holster and a Henry repeater. The item that received most of his attention though was the Bowie in the beaded sheath. He had seen that knife many times…it was Tye's. A volley of shots got his attention away from the table. Looking out the window he saw two of the men were firing into the cedars where he figured Tye was. While they were firing, the third man, Zach, was moving up the slope and when he dropped behind a boulder the firing stopped. He watched the two men reloading and then one of the men and Zach opened up while the heavy set Mexican began to climb the hill once more. By keeping Tye's head down while they closed the distance, Tye would be dead pretty damn quick.

He stood up and walked out on the porch and stood beside Lupe who sat in a chair watching the hill. His attention on the hill and not on Dan was a big mistake. Dan slipped his hand behind his back and felt for the knife he carried under his jacket in his belt. Finding it, in one swift motion he jerked the knife from his belt and drove it into the side of Lupe's neck and ripped it forward. The double edged blade ripped through the outlaw's jugular. Lupe grabbed his neck with both hands, blood gushing between his fingers. He looked up at Dan and tried to say something but only a crimson froth bubbled from his lips. The only sound was a gurgling sound as he choked on his own blood. His legs twitched a couple of times and his bloody hands fell to his sides as his life as an outlaw came to an end.

Dan went back inside the cantina to the table and picked up Tye's Bowie and guns. He walked outside to get a little closer to the hill. He found a water barrel and dropped behind it. He checked Tye's rifle to make sure it was loaded and then laid it across the top of the barrel pointed at the hill. In circumstances like this, unlike Tye, he had no qualms about shooting a man in the back. He sat down and took aim at the closest Mexican and fired. The bullet struck the man in the back. His arms went above his head and he fell back, tumbling down the slope for about ten feet before coming to rest against a big cactus.

He fired again at the big Mexican and heard the man curse, and grasped his left shoulder. He swung the gun toward the man he figured was Zach. He saw the man looking at him and then back up the slope and then back at him. He was in crossfire and knew he was a dead man if made an attempt to move. Dan held his fire because he knew if this was Zach, Tye wanted him alive. The man threw his gun down and stood up with his hands over his head. Dan stood up and hollered at Tye.

"TYE, ITS DAN AUGUST. COME OUT. He watched the stand of cedar and saw Tye stand up and start down the slope with a severe limp. When Tye was even with Zach he motioned the man to go down the hill. He walked over to the man he figured was Alvarez and stuck the rifle against his head. Alvarez looked up and Tye motioned for him to stand up and head down the hill. He had gone only a few steps when Dan shouted.

"BEHIND YOU TYE!"

Tye whirled around and in one motion brought the rifle up and fired. The Mexican that was coming down behind him clutched his belly and fell to his knees. He stayed on his knees for about five seconds and then fell on his face on the rocky slope and didn't move. Tye turned his attention back to Alvarez who appeared to be in a hell of lot of pain.

"You're a sight for sore eyes you damn worthless old scout," Tye said.

"Looks like this worthless old scout saved the famous one's butt this time," Dan said smiling.

"I'd say your timing was very good," Tye said and grabbed his friend's hand, shaking it vigorously.

They herded the two prisoners toward the cantina. Once inside, Tye headed to the bar and found some water. He downed three or four drinks quickly and immediately felt better. He grabbed a bottle of tequila and walked over to Dan and the prisoners. He held a gun on them while Dan tied their hands behind their backs. Alvarez screamed in pain when his arm was jerked back. Tye saw the hole in front of his shoulder and figure it had shattered his shoulder bone. When the men were bound Tye sat down and asked Dan to look at his wounds. Dan looked at the scab on his head and the two other wounds.

"Which one you want tended to first?"

"Don't get smart, just get a hot towel and see if you can clean them up a little."

The woman came out with hot water and a couple of towels. She walked over to Alvarez and slapped him hard across the face. She called him all kinds of names in Spanish. Her touch was gentle as she washed Tye's wounds and then the fun part came. Tye held his breath as Dan poured some tequila on the side of his head, shoulder and leg. Each time, Tye hollered and came out of the chair cursing. Dan just smiled. "Hurts some don't it partner," he said, listening to the scout curse him.

"What are we going to do with these two?" Dan asked.

"Alvarez has a lot to answer to for things he did a long time ago. Zach here is going to answer to me and then go back and face a horse stealing charge."

"What do you mean answer to you?" Zach asked. Tye limped over to him and got into his face.

"I'm going to see if you are as tough against a man as you are against a boy." He slapped Zach hard on the cheek. Zach strained against the rope that bound his hands.

"Cut me loose and I'll show you…you bastard."

Tye stepped back from the man and moved the table to make some room.

"Tye," Dan said. "You aren't going to do what I think you are…are you?"

Tye move another table. "You are in no shape to take this man on," Dan added.
"Wait until you wounds are healed and then do it."

"Turn him loose, Dan." Tye said. "Then step back."

Tye limped over to the big man.

Zach looked at Tye and laughed. "Hell man, this ain't going to be no fight. You barely can walk and." he never finished as Tye hit him the belly with a hard right fist that took the wind out of Zach. Tye stepped back to give Zach time to get his wind back. A minute later Zach looked like an infuriated bear as he charged Tye and head butted him in the stomach. Tye took the blow without losing his wind and fell back pulling the bear of a man with him and as he fell, bent, placed his left foot in Zach's stomach and when his back hit the floor he straightened his leg and Zach was somersaulted four or five feet in the air and hit the floor on his back, stunning him. Tye was up and on top of him before he could move and straddling the man's chest, begin pounding the man's face with rights and lefts. He grabbed him by the ears and bashed his head against the wooden floor. Zach was out cold. Tye stood up and looked at the smiling woman.

"Get me some water." He said in his best Spanish, which was poor at best. When she came back, he threw water in the man's bloody face. Zach shook his head and sputtered some and looked at Tye.

"Stand up you piece of shit," Tye said, having all his emotions come to the surface that had been building since he found out about Todd's beating.

"Why?" Zach said through bloody lips. He reached in his mouth and pulled out a tooth.

"Why what" Tye asked.

"Why did you follow me all the way here over a horse and a kid?"

"I could care less about the horse," he said as he reached down and pulled the man to his feet. "The boy was my nephew that you damn near beat to death."

Alvarez and Zach looked at each other. Alvarez shook his head and mumbled something in Spanish. Zach stood there swaying a little and took a swing at Tye's head which Tye blocked easily with his left arm and countered with a right which caught

Zach flush on the nose. Blood flowed freely down the man's face as he collapsed again.

"More water," Tye said.

"Tye...Tye," Dan said grabbing his friend. "He's done Tye. He's whipped worse than any man I have ever seen. Don't kill him because he will hang for horse stealing. Let's get him and Alvarez on their horses, get some supplies and get to the fort. You need some doctoring."

Tye sat down in a chair and for the first time in what seemed forever, relaxed.

Alvarez sat in a chair in excruciating pain with his shoulder; Zach was out cold on the floor, so Dan sat down beside his friend. Tye looked over at him and knowing he might have been dead if his friend had not showed up put his right hand on Dan's shoulder.

"Thanks Dan. Thanks for not only saving my tail but for keeping me from killing Zach. The last time I actually wanted to beat a man to death was the outlaw, Yancey Cates." Tye's breathing was back to normal and he was thinking, planning for the trip back. He took some coins out of his pocket and handed them to the woman. "Can you give me a bottle of tequila and some food to carry with us?" The woman, to both Dan's and Tye's surprise apparently understood because she nodded and left.

Second Chance

Tye walked to the stables and saw the man who he had bashed his head in the other night. The man and another one that was wounded was being escorted out of the village by some of the village men holding, hoes, pitchforks, and shovels as weapons. Sandy saw Tye coming and met him at the gate. After Sandy was through rubbing his head against his master's chest and nibbling on his hand, Tye found his saddle, blanket, saddle bags, and bridle. After saddling Sandy, he rode around to the cantina. He saw Dan holding the reins of Todd's horse. Tye was leading a good looking horse for Dan to ride. He figured it belonged to one of the dead outlaws.

"Here's you a ride, Dan. I don't think the previous owner will object."

They had their water and supplies, their prisoners were mounted and they were on their way back to Fort Clark. Tye cussed Dan one more time when he poured the tequila on his wounds and would a couple more times on the way back home.

EPILOGUE

The trip back to Fort Clark was uneventful except for the complaining of the two prisoners. Zach complained of the bruises on his face, the lost teeth and broken nose. Alvarez complained of his shoulder injury and that he was in constant pain. Tye's injuries were better, thanks to the tequila treatments.

They had stopped in the village where Pablo lived and Tye had a good visit with his friend. At Pablo's request he did not mention the man Pablo killed. There had been a couple of Pablo's friends present when Tye talked about the fight and how Pablo had saved him. Word spread quickly and the village now had a new hero-their own Pablo.

There was quite a celebration at Brackettville when the two scouts returned with not only Zach, but "The Ghost" also. The old timers knew who 'The Ghost" was and some taunted him with insults and talk of the hangman's noose and how it was going to feel around his neck.

Happiest of all, besides Rebecca and Todd was Major Thurston. He could not say enough about Tye and Dan and after hearing the full story, he said he would personally invite Pablo and his family to the fort for the party he planned to throw for Rebecca when the baby was born.

Tye was summoned to Thurston's office later that day. When he arrived he found Adam, shackles and all, there also. Tye shook his hand and sat in the chair beside the outlaw. Major Thurston stood up and walked to the window, standing there with his hands clasped behind his back staring out at the parade grounds. Without turning around and looking at the two men he spoke.

"I have been doing a lot of thinking about your situation, Mr. Carter. I know you saved Tye's and Wallace's lives the other day when you could have escaped. I know you regret what happened at the Rocking B Ranch." He turned around and looked at Adam whose hopes had risen with what he had just heard. Thurston continued talking as he walked toward the two men. "However, your recent actions do not change the fact that six people died because of what you did, two of them, a woman and a teenager who considered you family." Adam's hopes for anything good to come from this meeting dwindled. He was headed for a hanging or prison. "As Tye is aware there is no law here so I have to decide your fate and it's not an easy thing to do. There are a lot of good soldiers in this man's army, but I am not naïve enough to think all of them are necessarily good 'ole boys. I am sure some of my best ones have a questionable past and joined the army to escape the law. The army life is tough and it takes a tough man to handle it. You get two good meals a day and a roof over your head when you are here in the fort. On patrol, you get beans and jerky and a good chance of getting killed by bandits or the Apache." The major sat down and looked at the nervous Carter. "For your punishment for your crimes you will be forced to join this man army for a minimum of four years with no leave. The only time you will cross that bridge to leave the fort will be when you are on patrol."

Adams heart leaped for joy and tears clouded his eyes. He got control of his emotions and stood up. "Major Thurston, you have just given me a second chance at life and I promise you I will be the best damn soldier you and Tye have ever seen." He turned and gave a surprised Tye a hug, and then shook the Majors hand.

Thurston clasped his hand. "You will remain in the guardhouse until I can get the paper work completed." The guard stepped forward and escorted the happy soldier back to his cell.

"Thanks Major," Tye said. "I don't think you will regret it."

"I hope not. We'll see."

Todd had been reunited with his horse and no one could figure out who was happier, Todd or his horse, Lucky. Lucky trotted over to Todd when he saw him and nudged him in the chest with his nose a few times. Todd hugged his horses' neck, rubbing him under the chin. Both the boy and horse were as happy as two pigs in a sty.

Todd was pretty much over his beating and was anxiously waiting for Tye to get to feeling better so they could continue his 'education'. Reading tracks and sign meant they would be outside the fort and that meant more time with Lucky.

A few days later, Tye, Rebecca, and Buff were guests at the O'Malley's for dinner. Tye had to recount the events of the last few days and then O'Malley had the floor. He told of his newest recruit and how he had proved that he was going to be one hell of a soldier. "I gave him my best shot as far as verbal abuse and putting him down. He would just smile at me with those blue eyes and say, yes sir, Sergeant, Sir. You are right. I am worthless piece of horse dung and then he would laugh. I'd have to turn my head so he would not see me smile. I would say your man Adam, is going to be a top soldier.

After the meal and all the talk, the three of them, Tye, Rebecca, and Buff walked the short distance to their home. A feeling of contentment and love flowed freely between them as they discussed how life was going to be after the baby arrived. The big event was now less than a week away and everyone was anxious.

All was quiet at Fort Clark too…at least for now. But with the fort's history, Tye knew it was not going to be long before trouble showed its ugly head and he would be on scout once again. The more he thought about his situation with the new baby, the better the offer from the governor sounded about his becoming a U.S. Marshall. He had received a letter several months ago offering him the position. He was thirty years old and had no trade other than hunting, tracking, and fighting. He knew tracking down criminals would be dangerous but nothing like tracking Apaches.

"I need to do some serious thinking about my future…my family's future, he thought. *" I will talk to the major after the baby comes. I may need to go see the governor and see what the offer entails. "* He nodded his head, then another thought occurred. *" It's been along time since I received the letter. The offer may not even exist anymore. This is something Rebecca and I need to discuss, but not till after our baby arrives. "*

~~

Alvarez, alias *The Ghost,* was hung by the neck a week to the day after Tye brought him in for all his past crimes along the Border. Zach Robertson was sentenced to five years hard labor at the prison in San Antonio for the brutal beating of young Todd Jenkins and the theft of the young man's horse. He would be held in the guardhouse at Fort Clark until a marshal arrived to take him to San Antonio.

Second Chance

Three days later, Tye and Buff rushed Rebecca to the fort's hospital. Once Rebecca was there, Tye sent Buff to get Mrs. O'Malley. The big event that everyone on the fort had waited for was here.

Gary McMillan

Yahzie-

Apache Warrior

Book VIII of the Tye Watkins Series

The big event everyone on the fort had been waiting for was finally here; Rebecca and Tye's becoming parents. The happy occasion was short lived however. Two men, half dead, rode into Fort Clark with a story about one Apache who killed four of their friends and wounded both of them.

Their story was full of holes as far as Tye was concerned, but Major Thurston, Post Commander, dispatched his chief of scouts to find the Apache and bring him in-dead or alive. While on the trail of the Apache, Tye would find there was a reason for his killing the men.

Yahzie was a Mescalero Apache. The Mescalero was known to be the most fearsome of the Apache tribes. They were great warriors who were completely fearless in battle. Yahzie was known as a great warrior among his people. Tye would find that the Apache's reputation was understated. When the scout finally came face to face with Yahzie, he found himself in the biggest struggle for survival of his entire life.

Gary McMillan

I9780984473045
WESTERN MAC
McMillan, Gary.
Second chance /

CPSIA information can be obtained at www.ICGtesting.com
Printed in the USA
238182LV00009B/128/P

9 780984 473045